A high tree of blinding white grew quickly, soundlessly up the sky from behind South Ridge. Guards on the towers of Hallen Castle cried out, their small voices and clangor of warning were swallowed by the roar of sound, the hammerstroke of wind, the staggering of the forest.

Lord Mogien of Hallen met his guest on the run. "Was your ship behind South Ridge, Starlord Rocannon?"

Very white in the face, but quiet-voiced as usual, the other said, "It was."

They were all dead, all fourteen of them, his companions and his friends. And now there were enemies here, on this world—and he was alone. . . .

URSULA KROEBER LE GUIN, daughter of A. L. Kroeber (anthropologist) and Theodora Kroeber (author), was born in Berkeley, California in 1929. She attended college at Radcliffe and Columbia, and married C. A. LeGuin in Paris in 1951. The LeGuins and their three children live in Portland, Oregon.

Ursula LeGuin's novels include ROCANNON'S WORLD, PLANET OF EXILE, CITY OF ILLUSIONS and THE LEFT HAND OF DARKNESS, all published by Ace Books. THE LEFT HAND OF DARKNESS in particular attracted wide attention and strong praise; it was awarded both the Nebula and the Hugo Awards.

Rocannon's World

by

URSULA K. Le GUIN

A Division of Charter Communications Inc.
1120 Avenue of the Americas
New York, N.Y. 10036

ROCANNON'S WORLD

Printed in U.S.A.

PROLOGUE: THE NECKLACE

HOW CAN YOU TELL the legend from the fact on these worlds that lie so many years away?—planets without names, called by their people simply The World, planets without history, where the past is the matter of myth, and a returning explorer finds his own doings of a few years back have become the gestures of a god. Unreason darkens that gap of time bridged by our lightspeed ships, and in the darkness uncertainty and disproportion grow like weeds.

In trying to tell the story of a man, an ordinary League scientist, who went to such a nameless half-known world not many years ago, one feels like an archeologist amid millennial ruins, now struggling through choked tangles of leaf, flower, branch and vine to the sudden bright geometry of a wheel or a polished cornerstone, and now entering some commonplace, sunlit doorway to find inside it the darkness, the impossible flicker of a flame, the glitter of a jewel, the half-glimpsed movement of a woman's arm.

How can you tell fact from legend, truth from truth?

Through Rocannon's story the jewel, the blue glitter seen briefly, returns. With it let us begin, here:

Galactic Area 8, No. 62: FOMALHAUT II.
High-Intelligence Life Forms: Species Contacted:
Species I.

A) Gdemiar (singular Gdem): Highly intelligent, fully hominoid nocturnal troglodytes, 120-135 cm. in height, light skin, dark head-hair. When contacted these cave-dwellers possessed a rigidly stratified oli-

garchic urban society modified by partial colonial telephathy, and a technologically oriented Early Steel culture. Technology enhanced to Industrial, Point C, during League Mission of 252-254. In 254 an Automatic Drive ship (to-from New South Georgia) was presented to oligarchs of the Kiriensea Area community. Status C-Prime.

B) Fiia (singular Fian): Highly intelligent, fully hominoid, diurnal, av. ca. 130 cm. in height, observed individuals generally light in skin and hair. Brief contacts indicated village and nomadic communal societies, partial colonial telepathy, also some indication of short-range TK. The race appears a-technological and evasive, with minimal and fluid culture-patterns. Currently untaxable. Status E-Query.

Species II.

Liuar (singular Liu): Highly intelligent, fully hominoid, diurnal, av. height above 170 cm., this species possesses a fortress/village, clan-descent society, a blocked technology (Bronze), and feudal-heroic culture. Note horizontal social cleavage into 2 pseudo-races: (a: Olgyior, "midmen," light-skinned and dark-haired; (b: Angyar, "lords," very tall, dark-skinned, yellow-haired—

"That's her," said Rocannon, looking up from the *Abridged Handy Pocket Guide to Intelligent Life-forms* at the very tall, dark-skinned, yellow-haired woman who stood halfway down the long museum hall. She stood still and erect, crowned with bright hair, gazing at something in a display case. Around her fidgeted four uneasy and unattractive dwarves.

"I didn't know Fomalhaut II had all those people besides the trogs," said Ketho, the curator.

"I didn't either. There are even some "Unconfirmed" species listed here, that they never contacted. Sounds like time for a more thorough survey mission to the place. Well, now at least we know what she is."

"I wish there were some way of knowing *who* she is. . . ."

She was of an ancient family, a descendant of the first kings of the Angyar, and for all her poverty her hair shone with the pure, steadfast gold of her inheritance. The little people, the Fiia, bowed when she passed them, even when she was a barefoot child running in the fields, the light and fiery comet of her hair brightening the troubled winds of Kirien.

She was still very young when Durhal of Hallan saw her, courted her, and carried her away from the ruined towers and windy halls of her childhood to his own high home. In Hallan on the mountainside there was no comfort either, though splendor endured. The windows were unglassed, the stone floors bare; in coldyear one might wake to see the night's snow in long, low drifts beneath each window. Durhal's bride stood with narrow bare feet on the snowy floor, braiding up the fire of her hair and laughing at her young husband in the silver mirror that hung in their room. That mirror, and his mother's bridal-gown sewn with a thousand tiny crystals, were all his wealth. Some of his lesser kinfolk of Hallan still possessed wardrobes of brocaded clothing, furniture of gilded wood, silver harness for their steeds, armor and silver-mounted swords, jewels and jewelry—and on these last Durhal's bride looked enviously, glancing back at a gemmed coronet or a golden brooch even when the wearer of the ornament stood aside to let her pass, deferent to her birth and marriage-rank.

Fourth from the High Seat of Hallan Revel sat Durhal and his bride Semley, so close to Hallanlord that the old man often poured wine for Semley with his own hand, and spoke of hunting with his nephew and heir Durhal, looking on the young pair with a grim, unhopeful love. Hope came hard to the Angyar of Hallan and all the Western Lands, since the Starlords had appeared with their houses that leaped about on pillars of fire and their awful weapons that could level hills. They had interfered with all the old ways and wars, and though the sums were small there was terrible shame to the Angyar in having to pay a tax to them, a tribute for the Starlord's war that was to be fought with some strange enemy, somewhere in the hollow places between the stars, at the end of years. "It will be your war too," they said, but for a generation now the Angyar had sat in idle shame in their revelhalls, watching their double swords rust, their sons grow up without ever striking a blow in battle, their daughters marry poor men, even midmen, having no dowry of heroic loot to bring a noble husband. Hallanlord's face was bleak when he watched the fair-haired couple and heard their laughter as they drank bitter wine and joked together in the cold, ruinous, resplendent fortress of their race.

Semley's own face hardened when she looked down the hall and saw, in seats far below hers, even down among the halfbreeds and the midmen, against white skins and black hair, the gleam and flash of precious stones. She herself had brought nothing in dowry to her husband, not even a silver hairpin. The dress of a thousand crystals she had put away in a chest for the wedding-day of her daughter, if daughter it was to be.

It was, and they called her Haldre, and when the fuzz on her little brown skull grew longer it shone with steadfast gold, the inheritance of the lordly generations, the only gold she would ever possess. . . .

Semley did not speak to her husband of her discontent. For all his gentleness to her, Durhal in his hard lordly pride had only contempt for envy, for vain wishing, and she dreaded his contempt. But she spoke to Durhal's sister Durossa.

"My family had a great treasure once," she said. "It was a necklace all of gold, with the blue jewel set in the center—sapphire?"

Durossa shook her head, smiling, not sure of the name either. It was late in warmyear, as these Northern Angyar called the summer of the eight-hundred-day year, beginning the cycle of months anew at each equinox; to Semley it seemed an outlandish calendar, a midmannish reckoning. Her family was at an end, but it had been older and purer than the race of any of these northwestern marchlanders, who mixed too freely with the Olgyior. She sat with Durossa in the sunlight on a stone windowseat high up in the Great Tower, where the older woman's apartment was. Widowed young, childless, Durossa had been given in second marriage to Hallanlord, who was her father's brother. Since it was a kinmarriage and a second marriage on both sides she had not taken the title of Hallanlady, which Semley would some day bear; but she sat with the old lord in the High Seat and ruled with him his domains. Older than her brother Durhal, she was fond of his young wife, and delighted in the bright-haired baby Haldre.

"It was bought," Semley went on, "with all the money my forebear Leynen got when he conquered the Southern Fiefs—all the money from a whole kingdom, think of it, for one jewel! Oh, it would outshine anything here in Hallan, surely, even those crystals like koob-eggs your cousin Issar wears. It was so beautiful they gave it a name of its own; they called it the Eye of the Sea. My great-grandmother wore it."

"You never saw it?" the older woman asked lazily, gazing down at the green mountainslopes where long, long summer sent its hot and restless winds straying among the forests and whirling down white roads to the seacoast far away.

"It was lost before I was born."

"No, my father said it was stolen before the Starlords ever came to our realm. He wouldn't talk of it, but there was an old midwoman full of tales who always told me the Fiia would know where it was."

"Ah, the Fiia I should like to see!" said Durossa. "They're in so many songs and tales; why do they never come to the Western Lands?"

"Too high, too cold in winter, I think. They like the sunlight of the valleys of the south."

"Are they like the Clayfolk?"

"Those I've never seen; they keep away from us in the south. Aren't they white like midmen, and misformed? The Fiia are fair; they look like children, only thinner, and wiser. Oh, I wonder if they know where the necklace is, who stole it and where he hid it! Think, Durossa—if I could come into Hallan Revel and sit down by my husband with the wealth of a kingdom round my neck, and outshine the other women as he outshines all men!"

Durossa bent her head above the baby, who sat studying her own brown toes on a fur rug between her mother and aunt. "Semley is foolish," she murmured to the baby; "Semley who shines like a falling star, Semley whose husband loves no gold but the gold of her. . . ."

And Semley, looking out over the green slopes of summer toward the distant sea, was silent.

But when another coldyear had passed, and the Starlords had come again to collect their taxes for the war against the world's end—this time using a couple of dwarvish Clayfolk as interpreters, and so leaving all the Angyar humiliated to the point of rebellion—and another warmyear too was gone, and Haldre had grown into a lovely, chattering child, Semley brought her one morning to Durossa's sunlit room in the tower. Semley wore an old cloak of blue, and the hood covered her hair.

"Keep Haldre for me these few days, Durossa," she said, quick and calm. "I'm going south to Kirien."

"To see your father?"

"To find my inheritance. Your cousins of Harget Fief have been taunting Durhal. Even that halfbreed Parna can torment him, because Parna's wife has a satin coverlet for her bed, and a diamond earring, and three gowns, the dough-faced black-haired trollop! while Durhal's wife must patch her gown—"

"Is Durhal's pride in his wife, or what she wears?"

But Semley was not to be moved. "The Lords of Hallan

are becoming poor men in their own hall. I am going to bring my dowry to my lord, as one of my lineage should."

"Semley! Does Durhal know you're going?"

"My return will be a happy one—that much let him know," said young Semley, breaking for a moment into her joyful laugh; then she bent to kiss her daughter, turned and before Durossa could speak, was gone like a quick wind over the floors of sunlit stone.

Married women of the Angyar never rode for sport, and Semley had not been from Hallan since her marriage; so now, mounting the high saddle of a windsteed, she felt like a girl again, like the wild maiden she had been, riding half-broken steeds on the north wind over the fields of Kirien. The beast that bore her now down from the hills of Hallan was of finer breed, striped coat fitting sleek over hollow, buoyant bones, green eyes slitted against the wind, light and mighty wings sweeping up and down to either side of Semley, revealing and hiding, revealing and hiding the clouds above her and the hills below.

On the third morning she came to Kirien and stood again in the ruined courts. Her father had been drinking all night, and, just as in the old days, the morning sunlight poking through his fallen ceilings annoyed him, and the sight of his daughter only increased his annoyance. "What are you back for?" he growled, his swollen eyes glancing at her and away. The fiery hair of his youth was quenched, gray strands tangled on his skull. "Did the young Halla not marry you, and you've come sneaking home?"

"I am Durhal's wife. I came to get my dowry, father."

The drunkard growled in disgust; but she laughed at him so gently that he had to look at her again, wincing.

"Is it true, father, that the Fiia stole the necklace Eye of the Sea?"

"How do I know? Old tales. The thing was lost before I was born, I think. I wish I never had been. Ask the Fiia if you want to know. Go to them, go back to your husband. Leave me alone here. There's no room at Kirien for girls and gold and all the rest of the story. The story's over here; this is the fallen place, this is the empty hall. The sons of Leynen all are dead, their treasures are all lost. Go on your way, girl."

Gray and swollen as the web-spinner of ruined houses, he turned and went blundering toward the cellars where he hid from daylight.

Leading the striped windsteed of Hallan, Semley left her old home and walked down the steep hill, past the village of the midmen, who greeted her with sullen respect, on over fields and pastures where the great, wing-clipped, half-wild herilor grazed, to a valley that was green as a painted bowl and full to the brim with sunlight. In the deep of the valley lay the village of the Fiia, and as she descended leading her steed the little, slight people ran up toward her from their huts and gardens, laughing, calling out in faint, thin voices.

"Hail Halla's bride, Kirienlady, Windborne, Semley the Fair!"

They gave her lovely names and she liked to hear them, minding not at all their laughter; for they laughed at all they said. That was her own way, to speak and laugh. She stood tall in her long blue cloak among their swirling welcome.

"Hail Lightfolk, Sundwellers, Fiia friends of men!"

They took her down into the village and brought her into one of their airy houses, the tiny children chasing along behind. There was no telling the age of a Fian once he was grown; it was hard even to tell one from another and be sure, as they moved about quick as moths around a candle, that she spoke always to the same one. But it seemed that one of them talked with her for a while, as the others fed and petted her steed, and brought water for her to drink, and bowls of fruit from their gardens of little trees. "It was never the Fiia that stole the necklace of the Lords of Kirien!" cried the little man. "What would the Fiia do with gold, Lady? For us there is sunlight in warmyear, and in coldyear the remembrance of sunlight; the yellow fruit, the yellow leaves in end-season, the yellow hair of our lady of Kirien; no other gold."

"Then it was some midman stole the thing?"

Laughter rang long and faint about her. "How would a midman dare? O Lady of Kirien, how the great jewel was stolen no mortal knows, not man nor midman nor Fian nor any among the Seven Folk. Only dead minds know how it was lost, long ago when Kireley the Proud whose great-granddaughter is Semley walked alone by the caves of the sea. But it may be found perhaps among the Sun-haters."

"The Clayfolk?"

A louder burst of laughter, nervous.

"Sit with us, Semley, sunhaired, returned to us from the north." She sat with them to eat, and they were as pleased with her graciousness as she with theirs. But when they heard her repeat that she would go to the Clayfolk to find her inheritance, if it was there, they began not to laugh; and little by little there were fewer of them around her. She was alone at last with perhaps the one she had spoken with before the meal. "Do not go among the Clayfolk, Semley," he said, and for a moment her heart failed her. The Fian, drawing his hand down slowly over his eyes, had darkened all the air about them. Fruit lay ash-white on the plate; all the bowls of clear water were empty. "In the mountains of the far land the Fiia and the Gdemiar parted. Long ago we parted," said the slight, still man of the Fiia. "Longer ago we were one. What we are not, they are. What we are, they are not. Think of the sunlight and the grass and the trees that bear fruit, Semley; think that not all roads that lead down lead up as well."

The Fian bowed, laughing a little.

Outside the village she mounted her striped windsteed, and, calling farewell in answer to their calling, rose up into the wind of afternoon and flew southwestward toward the caves down by the rocky shores of Kiriensea.

She feared she might have to walk far into those tunnel-caves to find the people she sought, for it was said the

Clayfolk never came out of their caves into the light of the sun, and feared even the Greatstar and the moons. It was a long ride; she landed once to let her steed hunt tree-rats while she ate a little bread from her saddle-bag. The bread was hard and dry by now and tasted of leather, yet kept a faint savor of its making, so that for a moment, eating it alone in a glade of the southern forests, she heard the quiet tone of a voice and saw Durhal's face turned to her in the light of the candles of Hallan. For a while she sat daydreaming of that stern and vivid young face, and of what she would say to him when she came home with a kingdom's ransom around her neck: "I wanted a gift worthy of my husband, Lord . . ." Then she pressed on, but when she reached the coast the sun had set, with the Greatstar sinking behind it. A mean wind had come up from the west, starting and gusting and veering, and her windsteed was weary fighting it. She let him glide down on the sand. At once he folded his wings and curled his thick, light limbs under him with a thrum of purring. Semley stood holding her cloak close at her throat, stroking the steed's neck so that he flicked his ears and purred again. The warm fur comforted her hand, but all that met her eyes was gray sky full of smears of cloud, gray sea, dark sand. And then running over the sand a low, dark creature—another—a group of them, squatting and running and stopping.

She called aloud to them. Though they had not seemed to see her, now in a moment they were all around her. They kept a distance from her windsteed; he had stopped purring, and his fur rose a little under Semley's hand. She took up the reins, glad of his protection but afraid of the nervous ferocity he might display. The strange folk stood silent, staring, their thick bare feet planted in the sand. There was no mistaking them: they were the height of the Fiia and in all else a shadow, a black image of those laughing people. Naked, squat, stiff, with lank black hair and gray-white skins, dampish looking like the skins of grubs; eyes like rocks.

"You are the Clayfolk?"

"Gdemiar are we, people of the Lords of the Realms of Night." The voice was unexpectedly loud and deep, and rang out pompous through the salt, blowing dusk; but, as with the Fiia, Semley was not sure which one had spoken.

"I greet you, Nightlords. I am Semley of Kirien, Durhal's wife of Hallan. I come to you seeking my inheritance, the necklace called Eye of the Sea, lost long ago."

"Why do you seek it here, Angya? Here is only sand and salt and night."

"Because lost things are known of in deep places," said Semley, quite ready for a play of wits, "and gold that came from earth has a way of going back to the earth. And sometimes the made, they say, returns to the maker." This last was a guess; it hit the mark.

"It is true the necklace Eye of the Sea is known to us by name. It was made in our caves long ago, and sold by us to the Angyar. And the blue stone came from the Clayfields of our kin to the east. But these are very old tales, Angya."

"May I listen to them in the places where they are told?"

The squat people were silent a while, as if in doubt. The gray wind blew by over the sand, darkening as the Greatstar set; the sound of the sea loudened and lessened. The deep voice spoke again: "Yes, lady of the Angyar. You may enter the Deep Halls. Come with us now." There was a changed note in his voice, wheedling. Semley would not hear it. She followed the Claymen over the sand, leading on a short rein her sharp-taloned steed.

At the cave-mouth, a toothless, yawning mouth from which a stinking warmth sighed out, one of the Claymen said, "The air-beast cannot come in."

"Yes," said Semley.

"No," said the squat people.

"Yes, I will not leave him here. He is not mine to leave. He will not harm you, so long as I hold his reins."

"No," deep voices repeated; but others broke in, "As

you will," and after a moment of hesitation they went on. The cave-mouth seemed to snap shut behind them, so dark was it under the stone. They went in single file, Semley last.

The darkness of the tunnel lightened, and they came under a ball of weak white fire hanging from the roof. Farther on was another, and another; between them long black worms hung in festoons from the rock. As they went on these fire-globes were set closer, so that all the tunnel was lit with a bright, cold light.

Semley's guides stopped at a parting of three tunnels, all blocked by doors that looked to be of iron. "We shall wait, Angya," they said, and eight of them stayed with her, while three others unlocked one of the doors and passed through. It fell to behind them with a clash.

Straight and still stood the daughter of the Angyar in the white, blank light of the lamps; her windsteed crouched beside her, flicking the tip of his striped tail, his great folded wings stirring again and again with the checked impulse to fly. In the tunnel behind Semley the eight Claymen squatted on their hams, muttering to one another in their deep voices, in their own tongue.

The central door swung clanging open. "Let the Angya enter the Realm of Night!" cried a new voice, booming and boastful. A Clayman who wore some clothing on his thick gray body stood in the doorway beckoning to her. "Enter and behold the wonders of our lands, the marvels made by hands, the works of the Nightlords!"

Silent, with a tug at her steed's reins, Semley bowed her head and followed him under the low doorway made for dwarfish fold. Another glaring tunnel stretched ahead, dank walls dazzling in the white light, but, instead of a way to walk upon, its floor carried two bars of polished iron stretching off side as far as she could see. On the bars rested some kind of cart with metal wheels. Obeying her new guide's gestures, with no hesitation and no trace of wonder on her face, Semley stepped into the cart and made the windsteed crouch beside her. The Clayman got in and sat down in front of her, moving bars and wheels about. A loud grinding noise arose, and a screaming of metal on metal, and then the walls of the tunnel began to jerk by. Faster and faster the walls slid past, till the fire-globes overhead ran into a blur, and the stale warm air became a foul wind blowing the hood back off her hair.

The cart stopped. Semley followed the guide up basalt steps into a vast anteroom and then a still vaster hall, carved by ancient waters or by the burrowing Clayfish out of the rock, its darkness that had never known sunlight lit with the uncanny cold brilliance of the globes. In grilles cut in the walls huge blades turned and turned, changing the stale air. The great closed space hummed and boomed with noise, the loud voices of the Clayfolk, the grinding and shrill buzzing and vibration of turning blades and wheels, the echoes and re-echoes of all this from the rock. Here all the stumpy figures of the Claymen were clothed in garments imitating those of the Starlords—divided trousers, soft boots, and hooded tunics—though the few women to be seen, hurrying servile dwarves, were naked. Of the males many were soldiers, bearing at their sides weapons shaped like the terrible light-throwers of the Starlords, though even Semley could see these were merely shaped iron clubs. What she saw, she saw without looking. She followed where she was led, turning her head neither to left nor right. When she came before a group of Claymen who wore iron circlets on their black hair her guide halted, bowed, boomed out, "The High Lords of the Gdemiar!"

There were seven of them, and all looked up at her with such arrogance on their lumpy gray faces that she wanted to laugh.

"I come among you seeking the lost treasure of my family, O Lords of the Dark Realm," she said gravely to them. "I seek Leynen's prize, the Eye of the Sea." Her voice was faint in the racket of the huge vault.

"So said our messengers, Lady Semley." This time she could pick out the one who spoke, one even shorter than the others, hardly reaching Semley's breast, with a white, powerful fierce face. "We do not have this thing you seek."

"Once you had it, it is said."

"Much is said, up there where the sun blinks."

"And words are borne off by the winds, where there are winds to blow. I do not ask how the necklace was lost to us and returned to you, its makers of old. Those are old tales, old grudges. I only seek to find it now. You do not have it now; but it may be you know where it is."

"It is not here."

"Then it is elsewhere."

"It is where you cannot come to it. Never, unless we help you."

"Then help me. I ask this as your guest."

"It is said, *The Angyar take; the Fiia give; the Gdemiar give and take*. If we do this for you, what will you give us?"

"My thanks, Nightlord."

She stood tall and bright among them, smiling. They all stared at her with a heavy, grudging wonder, a sullen yearning.

"Listen, Angya, this is a great favor you ask of us. You do not know how great a favor. You cannot understand. You are of a race that will not understand, that cares for nothing but windriding and crop-raising and sword-fighting and shouting together. But who made your swords of the bright steel? We, the Gdemiar! Your lords come to us here and in Clayfields and buy their swords and go away, not looking, not understanding. But you are here now, you will look, you can see a few of our endless marvels, the lights that burn forever, the car that pulls itself, the machines that make our clothes and cook our food and sweeten our air and serve us in all things. Know that all these things are beyond your understanding. And know this: we, the Gdemiar, are the friends of those you call the Starlords! We came with them to Hallan, to Reohan, to Hul-Orren, to all your castles, to help them speak to you. The lords to whom you, the proud Angyar, pay tribute, are our friends. They do us favors as we do them favors! Now, what do your thanks mean to us?"

"That is your question to answer," said Semley, "not mine. I have asked my question. Answer it, Lord."

For a while the seven conferred together, by word and silence. They would glance at her and look away, and mutter and be still. A crowd grew around them, drawn slowly and silently, one after another till Semley was encircled by hundreds of the matted black heads, and all the great booming cavern floor was covered with people, except a little space directly around her. Her windsteed was quivering with fear and irritation too long controlled, and his eyes had gone very wide and pale, like the eyes of a steed forced to fly at night. She stroked the warm fur of his head, whispering, "Quietly now, brave one, bright one, windlord. . . ."

"Angya, we will take you to the place where the treasure lies." The Clayman with the white face and iron crown had turned to her once more. "More than that we cannot do. You must come with us to claim the necklace where it lies, from those who keep it. The air-beast cannot come with you. You must come alone."

"How far a journey, Lord?"

His lips drew back and back. "A very far journey, Lady. Yet it will last only one long night."

"I thank you for your courtesy. Will my steed be well cared for this night? No ill must come to him."

"He will sleep till you return. A greater windsteed you will have ridden, when you see that beast again! Will you not ask where we take you?"

"Can we go soon on this journey? I would not stay long away from my home."

"Yes. Soon." Again the gray lips widened as he stared up into her face.

What was done in those next hours Semley could not have retold; it was all haste, jumble, noise, strangeness. While she held her steed's head a Clayman stuck a long needle into the golden-striped haunch. She nearly cried out at the sight, but her steed merely twitched and then, purring, fell asleep. He was carried off by a group of Clayfolk who clearly had to summon up their courage to touch his warm fur. Later on she had to see a needle driven into her own arm—perhaps to test her courage, she thought, for it did not seem to make her sleep; though she was not quite sure. There were times she had to travel in the rail-carts, passing iron doors and vaulted caverns by the hundred and hundred; once the rail-cart ran through a cavern that stretched off on either hand measureless into the dark, and all that darkness was full of great flocks of herilor. She could hear their cooing, husky calls, and glimpse the flocks in the front-lights of the cart; then she saw some more clearly in the white light, and saw that they were all wingless, and all blind. At that she shut her eyes. But there were more tunnels to go through, and always more caverns, more gray lumpy bodies and fierce faces and booming boasting voices, until at last they led her suddenly out into the open air. It was full night; she raised her eyes joyfully to the stars and the single moon shining, little Heliki brightening in the west. But the Clayfolk were all about her still, making her climb now into some new kind of cart or cave, she did not know which. It was small, full of little blinking lights like rushlights, very narrow and shining after the great dank caverns and the starlit night. Now another needle was stuck in her, and they told her she would have to be tied down in a sort of flat chair, tied down head and hand and foot.

"I will not," said Semley.

But when she saw that the four Claymen who were to be her guides let themselves be tied down first, she submitted. The others left. There was a roaring sound, and a long silence; a great weight that could not be seen pressed upon her. Then there was no weight; no sound; nothing at all.

"Am I dead?" asked Semley.

"Oh no, Lady," said a voice she did not like.

Opening her eyes, she saw the white face bent over her,

the wide lips pulled back, the eyes like little stones. Her bonds had fallen away from her, and she leaped up. She was weightless, bodiless; she felt herself only a gust of terror on the wind.

"We will not hurt you," said the sullen voice or voices. "Only let us touch you, Lady. We would like to touch your hair. Let us touch your hair. . . ."

The round cart they were in trembled a little. Outside its one window lay blank night, or was it mist, or nothing at all? One long night, they had said. Very long. She sat motionless and endured the touch of their heavy gray hands on her hair. Later they would touch her hands and feet and arms, and one her throat: at that she set her teeth and stood up, and they drew back.

"We have not hurt you, Lady," they said. She shook her head.

When they bade her, she lay down again in the chair that bound her down; and when light flashed golden, at the window, she would have wept at the sight, but fainted first.

"Well," said Rocannon, "now at least we know what she is."

"I wish there were some way of knowing *who* she is," the curator mumbled. "She wants something we've got here in the Museum, is that what the trogs say?"

"Now, don't call 'em trogs," Rocannon said conscientiously; as a hilfer, an ethnologist of the High Intelligence Life Forms, he was supposed to resist such words. "They're not pretty, but they're Status C Allies . . . I wonder why the Commission picked them to develop? Before even contacting all the HILF species? I'll bet the survey was from Centaurus—Centaurans always like nocturnals and cave-dwellers. I'd have backed Species II, here, I think."

The troglodytes seem to be rather in awe of her."

"Aren't you?"

Ketho glanced at the tall woman again, then reddened and laughed. "Well, in a way. I never saw such a beautiful alien type in eighteen years here on New South Georgia. I never saw such a beautiful woman anywhere, in fact. She looks like a goddess." The red now reached the top of his bald head, for Ketho was a shy curator, not given to hyperbole. But Rocannon nodded soberly, agreeing.

"I wish we could talk to her without those tr— Gdemiar as interpreters. But there's no help for it." Rocannon went toward their visitor, and when she turned her splendid face to him he bowed down very deeply, going right down to to the floor on one knee, his head bowed and his eyes shut. This was what he called his All-purpose Intercultural Curtsey, and he performed it with some grace. When he came erect again the beautiful woman smiled and spoke.

"She say, Hail, Lord of Stars," growled one of her squat escorts in Pidgin-Galactic.

"Hail, Lady of the Angyar," Rocannon replied. "In what way can we of the Museum serve the lady?"

Across the troglodytes' growling her voice ran like a brief silver wind.

"She say, Please give her necklace which treasure her blood-kin-forebears long long."

"Which necklace?" he asked, and understanding him, she pointed to the central display of the case before them, a magnificent thing, a chain of yellow gold, massive but very delicate in workmanship, set with one big hot-blue sapphire. Rocannon's eyebrows went up, and Ketho at his shoulder murmured, "She's got good taste. That's the Fomalhaut Necklace—famous bit of work."

She smiled at the two men, and again spoke to them over the heads of the troglodytes.

"She say, O Starlords, Elder and Younger Dwellers in House of Treasures, this treasure her one. Long long time. Thank you."

"How did we get the thing, Ketho?"

"Wait; let me look it up in the catalogue. I've got it here. Here. It came from these trogs—trolls—whatever they are: Gdemiar. They have a bargain-obsession, it says;

we had to let 'em buy the ship they came here on, an AD-4. This was part payment. It's their own handiwork."

"And I'll bet they can't do this kind of work anymore, since they've been steered to Industrial."

"But they seem to feel the thing is hers, not theirs or ours. It must be important, Rocanno, or they wouldn't have given up this time-span to her errand. Why, the objective lapse between here and Fomalhaut must be considerable!"

"Several years, no doubt," said the hilfer, who was used to starjumping. "Not very far. Well, neither the *Handbook* nor the *Guide* gives me enough data to base a decent guess on. These species obviously haven't been properly studied at all. The little fellows may be showing her simple courtesy. Or an interspecies war may depend on this damn sapphire. Perhaps her desire rules them, because they consider themselves totally inferior to her. Or despite appearances she may be their prisoner, their decoy. How can we tell? . . . Can you give the things away, Ketho?"

"Oh yes. All the Exotica are technically on loan, not our property, since these claims come up now and then. We seldom argue. Peace above all, until the War comes. . . ."

"Then I'd say give it to her."

Ketho smiled. "It's a privilege," he said. Unlocking the case, he lifted out the great golden chain; then, in his shyness, he held it out to Rocannon, saying, "You give it to her."

So the blue jewel first lay, for a moment, in Rocannon's hand.

His mind was not on it; he turned straight to the beautiful, alien woman, with his handful of blue fire and gold. She did not raise her hands to take it, but bent her head, and he slipped the necklace over her hair. It lay like a burning fuse along her golden-brown throat. She looked up from it with such pride, delight, and gratitude in her face that Rocannon stood wordless, and the little curator murmured hurriedly in his own language, "You're welcome, you're very welcome." She bowed her golden head to him and to Rocannon. Then, turning, she nodded to her squat guards—or captors?—and, drawing her worn blue cloak about her, paced down the long hall and was gone. Ketho and Rocannon stood looking after her.

"What I feel . . ." Rocannon began.

"Well?" Ketho inquired hoarsely, after a long pause.

"What I feel sometimes is that I . . . meeting these people from worlds we know so little of, you know, sometimes . . . that I have as it were blundered through the corner of a legend, of a tragic myth, maybe, which I do not understand. . . ."

"Yes," said the curator, clearing his throat. "I wonder . . . I wonder what her name is."

Semley the Fair, Semley the Golden, Semley of the Necklace. The Clayfolk had bent to her will, and so had even the Starlords in that terrible place where the Clayfolk had taken her, the city at the end of the night. They had bowed to her, and given her gladly her treasure from amongst their own.

But she could not yet shake off the feeling of those caverns about her where rock lowered overhead, where you could not tell who spoke or what they did, where voices boomed and gray hands reached out—Enough of that. She had paid for the necklace; very well. Now it was hers. The price was paid, the past was the past.

Her windsteed had crept out of some kind of box, with his eyes filmy and his fur rimed with ice, and at first when they had left the caves of the Gdemiar he would not fly. Now he seemed all right again, riding a smooth south wind through the bright sky toward Hallan. "Go quick, go quick," she told him, beginning to laugh as the wind cleared away her mind's darkness. "I want to see Durhal soon, soon. . . ."

And swiftly they flew, coming to Hallan by dusk of the second day. Now the caves of the Clayfolk seemed no more than last year's nightmare, as the steed swooped with her up the thousand steps of Hallan and across the

Chasmbridge where the forests fell away for a thousand feet. In the gold light of evening in the flightcourt she dismounted and walked up the last steps between the stiff cavern figures of heroes and the two gatewards, who bowed to her, staring at the beautiful, fiery thing around her neck.

In the Forehall she stopped a passing girl, a very pretty girl, by her looks one of Durhal's close kin, though Semley could not call to mind her name. "Do you know me, maiden? I am Semley Durhal's wife. Will you go tell the Lady Durossa that I have come back?"

For she was afraid to go on in and perhaps face Durhal at once, alone; she wanted Durossa's support.

The girl was gazing at her, her face very strange. But she murmured, "Yes, Lady," and darted off toward the Tower.

Semley stood waiting in the gilt, ruinous hall. No one came by; were they all at table in the Revelhall? The silence was uneasy. After a minute Semley started toward the stairs to the Tower. But an old woman was coming to her across the stone floor, holding her arms out, weeping.

"Oh Semley, Semley!"

She had never seen the gray-haired woman, and shrank back.

"But Lady, who are you?"

"I am Durossa, Semley."

She was quiet and still, all the time that Durossa embraced her and wept, and asked if it were true the Clayfolk had captured her and kept her under a spell all these long years, or had it been the Fiia with their strange arts? Then, drawing back a little, Durossa ceased to weep.

"You're still young, Semley. Young as the day you left here. And you wear round your neck the necklace. . . ."

"I have brought my gift to my husband Durhal. Where is he?"

"Durhal is dead."

Semley stood unmoving.

"Your husband, my brother, Durhal Hallanlord was killed seven years ago in battle. Nine years you had been gone. The Starlords came no more. We fell to warning with the Eastern Halls, with the Angyar of Log and Hul-Orren. Durhal, fighting, was killed by a midman's spear, for he had little armor for his body, and none at all for his spirit. He lies buried in the fields above Orren Marsh."

Semley turned away. "I will go to him, then," she said, putting her hand on the gold chain that weighed down her neck. "I will give him my gift."

"Wait, Semley! Durhal's daughter, your daughter, see her now, Haldre the Beautiful!"

It was the girl she had first spoken to and sent to Durossa, a girl of nineteen or so, with eyes like Durhal's eyes, dark blue. She stood beside Durossa, gazing with those steady eyes at this woman Semley who was her mother and was her own age. Their age was the same, and their gold hair, and their beauty. Only Semley was a little taller, and wore the blue stone on her breast.

"Take it, take it. It was for Durhal and Haldre that I brought it from the end of the long night!" Semley cried this aloud, twisting and bowing her head to get the heavy chain off, dropping the necklace so it fell on the stones with a cold, liquid clash. "O take it, Haldre!" she cried again, and then, weeping aloud, turned and ran from Hallan, over the bridge and down the long, broad steps, and, darting off eastward into the forest of the mountainside like some wild thing escaping, was gone.

PART ONE: The Starlord

I

So ends the first part of the legend; and all of it is true. Now for some facts, which are equally true, from the League *Handbook for Galactic Area Eight.*

Number 62: FOMALHAUT II.

Type AE—Carbon Life. An iron-core planet, diameter 6600 miles, with heavy oxygen-rich atmosphere. Revolution: 800 Earthdays 8 hrs. 11 min. 42 sec. Rotation: 29 hrs. 51 min. 02 sec. Mean distance from sun 3.2 AU, orbital eccentricity slight. Obliquity of ecliptic 27° 20′ 20″ causing marked seasonal change. Gravity .86 Standard.

Four major landmasses, Northwest, Southwest, East and Antarctic Continents, occupy 38% of planetary surface.

Four satellites (types Perner, Loklik, R-2 and Phobos). The Companion of Fomalhaut is visible as a superbright star.

Nearest League World: New South Georgia, capital Kerguelen (7.88 lt. yrs.).

History: The planet was charted by the Elieson Expedition in 202, robot-probed in 218.

First Geographical Survey, 235-6. Director: J. Kiolaf. The major landmasses were surveyed by air (see maps 3114-a, b, c, 3115-a, b.). Landings, geological and biological studies and HILF contacts were made only on East and Northwest Continents (see description of intelligent species below).

Technological Enhancement Mission to Species I-A, 252-4. Director: J. Kiolaf (Northwest Continent only.)

Control and Taxation Missions to Species I-A and II were carried out under auspices of the Area Foundation in Kerguelen, N.S.Ga., in 254, 258, 262, 266, 270; in 275 the planet was placed under Interdict by the Allworld HILF Authority, pending more adequate study of its intelligent species.

First Ethnographic Survey, 321. Director: G. Rocannon.

A high tree of blinding white grew quickly, soundlessly up the sky from behind South Ridge. Guards on the towers of Hallan Castle cried out, striking bronze on bronze. Their small voices and clangor of warning were swallowed by the roar of sound, the hammerstroke of wind, the staggering of the forest.

Mogien of Hallan met his guest the Starlord on the run, heading for the flightcourt of the castle. "Was your ship behind South Ridge, Starlord?"

Very white in the face, but quiet-voiced as usual, the other said, "It was."

"Come with me." Mogien took his guest on the postillion saddle of the windsteed that waited ready saddled in the flightcourt. Down the thousand steps, across the Chasmbridge, off over the sloping forests of the domain of Hallan the steed flew like a gray leaf on the wind.

As it crossed over South Ridge the riders saw smoke rise blue through the level gold lances of the first sunlight. A forest fire was fizzling out among damp, cool thickets in the streambed of the mountainside.

Suddenly beneath them a hole dropped away in the side of the hills, a black pit filled with smoking black dust. At the edge of the wide circle of annihilation lay trees burnt to long smears of charcoal, all pointing their fallen tops away from the pit of blackness.

The young Lord of Hallan held his gray steed steady on the updraft from the wrecked valley and stared down, saying nothing. There were old tales from his grandfather's and great-grandfather's time of the first coming of the Starlords, how they had burnt away hills and made the sea boil with their terrible weapons, and with the threat of those weapons had forced all the Lords of Angien to pledge them fealty and tribute. For the first time now Mogien believed those tales. His breath was stuck in his throat for a second. "Your ship was . . ."

"The ship was here. I was to meet the others here, today. Lord Mogien, tell your people to avoid this place. For a while. Till after the rains, next coldyear."

"A spell?"

"A poison. Rain will rid the land of it." The Starlord's voice was still quiet, but he was looking down, and all at once he began to speak again, not to Mogien but to that black pit beneath them, now striped with the bright early sunlight. Mogien understood no word he said, for he spoke in his own tongue, the speech of the Starlords; and there was no man now in Angien or all the world who spoke that tongue.

The young Angya checked his nervous mount. Behind him the Starlord drew a deep breath and said, "Let's go back to Hallan. There is nothing here. . . ."

The steed wheeled over the smoking slopes. "Lord Rokanan, if your people are at war now among the stars, I pledge in your defense the swords of Hallan!"

"I thank you, Lord Mogien," said the Starlord, clinging to the saddle, the wind of their flight whipping at his bowed graying head.

The long day passed. The night wind gusted at the casements of his room in the tower of Hallan Castle, making the fire in the wide hearth flicker. Coldyear was nearly over; the restlessness of spring was in the wind. When he raised his head he smelled the sweet musty fragrance of grass tapestries hung on the walls and the sweet fresh fragrance of night in the forests outside. He spoke into his transmitter once more: "Rocannon here. This is Rocannon. Can you answer?" He listened to the silence of the receiver a long time, then once more tried ship frequency: "Rocannon here . . ." When he noticed how low he was speaking, almost whispering, he stopped and cut off the set. They were dead, all fourteen of them, his companions and his friends. They had all been on Fomalhaut II for half one of the planet's long years, and it had been time for them to confer and compare notes. So Smate and his crew had come around from East Continent, and picked up the Arctic crew on the way, and and ended up back here to meet with Rocannon, the Director of the First Ethnographic Survey, the man who had brought them all here. And now they were dead.

And their work—all their notes, pictures, tapes, all that would have justified their death to them—that was all gone too, blown to dust with them, wasted with them.

Rocannon turned on his radio again to Emergency frequency; but he did not pick up the transmitter. To call was only to tell the enemy that there was a survivor. He sat still. When a resounding knock came at his door he said in the strange tongue he would have to speak from now on, "Come in!"

In strode the young Lord of Hallan, Mogien, who had been his best informant for the culture and mores of Species II, and who now controlled his fate. Mogien was very tall, like all his people, bright-haired and dark-skinned, his handsome face schooled to a stern calm through which sometimes broke the lightning of powerful emotions: anger, ambition, joy. He was followed by his Olgyior servant Raho, who set down a yellow flask and two cups on a chest, poured the cups full, and withdrew. The heir of Hallan spoke: "I would drink with you, Starlord."

"And my kin with yours and our sons together, Lord," replied the ethnologist, who had not lived on nine different exotic planets without learning the value of good manners.

He and Mogien raised their wooden cups bound with silver and drank.

"The wordbox," Mogien said, looking at the radio, "it will not speak again."

"Not with my friends' voices."

Mogien's walnut-dark face showed no feeling, but he said, "Lord Rokanan, the weapon that killed them, this is beyond all imagining."

"The League of All Worlds keeps such weapons for use in the War To Come. Not against our own worlds."

"Is this the War, then?"

"I think not. Yaddam, whom you knew, was staying with the ship; he would have heard news of that on the ansible in the ship, and radioed me at once. There would have been warning. This must be a rebellion against the League. There was rebellion brewing on a world called Faraday when I left Kerguelen, and by sun's time that was nine years ago."

"This little wordbox cannot speak to the City Kerguelen?"

"No; and even if it did, it would take the words eight years to go there, and the answer eight years to come back to me." Rocannon spoke with his usual grave and simple politeness, but his voice was a little dull as he explained his exile. "You remember the ansible, the big machine I showed you in the ship, which can speak instantly to other worlds, with no loss of years—it was that that they were after, I expect. It was only bad luck that my friends were all at the ship with it. Without it I can do nothing."

"But if your kinfolk, your friends, in the City Kerguelen, call you on the ansible, and there is no answer, will they not come to see—" Mogien saw the answer as Rocannon said it:

"In eight years. . . ."

When he had shown Mogien over the Survey ship, and shown him the instantaneous trasmitter, the ansible, Rocannon had told him also about the new kind of ship that could go from one star to another in no time at all.

"Was the ship that killed your friends an FTL?" inquired the Angyar warlord.

"No. It was manned. There are enemies here, on this world, now."

This became clear to Mogien when he recalled that Rocannon had told him that living creatures could not ride the FTL ships and live; they were used only as robot-bombers, weapons that could appear and strike and vanish all within a moment. It was a queer story, but no queerer than the story Mogien knew to be true: that, though the kind of ship Rocannon had come here on took years and years to ride the night between the worlds, those years to the men in the ship seemed only a few hours. In the City Kerguelen on the star Forrosul this man Rocannon had spoken to Semley of Hallan and given her the jewel Eye of the Sea, nearly half a hundred years ago. Semley who had lived sixteen years in one night was long dead, her daughter Haldre was an old woman, her grandson Mogien a grown man; yet here sat Rocannon, who was not old. Those years had passed, for him, in riding between the stars. It was very strange, but there were other tales stranger yet.

"When my mother's mother Semley rode across the night . . ." Mogien began, and paused.

"There was never so fair a lady in all the worlds," said the Starlord, his face less sorrowful for a moment.

"The lord who befriended her is welcome among her kinfolk," said Mogien. "But I meant to ask, Lord, what ship she rode. Was it ever taken from the Clayfolk? Does it have the ansible on it, so you could tell your kinfolk of this enemy?"

For a second Rocannon looked thunderstruck, then he calmed down. "No," he said, "it doesn't. It was given to the Clayfolk seventy years ago; there was no instantaneous transmission then. And it would have been installed recently, because the planet's been under Interdict for forty-five years now. Due to me. Because I interfered. Because, after I met Lady Semley, I went to my people and said. What are we doing on this world we don't know anything about? Why are we taking their money and pushing them about? What right have we? But if I'd left the situation alone at least there'd be someone coming here every couple of years; you wouldn't be completely at the mercy of this invader—"

"What does an invader want with us?" Mogien inquired, not modestly, but curiously.

"He wants your planet, I suppose. Your world. Your earth. Perhaps yourselves as slaves. I don't know."

"If the Clayfolk still have that ship, Rokanan, and if the ship goes to the City, you could go, and rejoin your people."

The Starlord looked at him a minute. "I suppose I could," he said. His tone was dull again. There was silence between them for a minute longer, and then Rocannon spoke with passion: "I left you people open to this. I brought my own people into it and they're dead. I'm not going to run off eight years into the future and find out what happened next! Listen, Lord Mogien, if you could help me get south to the Clayfolk, I might get the ship and use it here on the planet, scout about with it. At least, if I can't change its automatic drive, I can send it off to Kerguelen with a message. But I'll stay here."

"Semley found it, the tale tells, in the caves of the Gdemiar near the Kiriensea."

"Will you lend me a windsteed, Lord Mogien?"

"And my company, if you will."

"With thanks!"

"The Clayfolk are bad hosts to lone guests," said Mogien, looking pleased. Not even the thought of that ghastly black hole blown in the mountainside could quell the itch in the two long swords hitched to Mogien's belt. It had been a long time since the last foray.

"May our enemy die without sons," the Angya said gravely, raising his refilled cup.

Rocannon, whose friends had been killed without warning in an unarmed ship, did not hesitate. "May they die without sons," he said, and drank with Mogien, there in the yellow light of rushlights and double moon, in the High Tower of Hallan.

II

BY EVENING of the second Rocannon was stiff and windburned, but had learned to sit easy in the high saddle and to guide with some skill the great flying beast from Hallan stables. Now the pink air of the long, slow sunset stretched above and beneath him, levels of rose-crystal light. The windsteeds were flying high to stay as long as they could in sunlight, for like great cats they loved warmth. Mogien on his black hunter—a stallion, would you call it, Rocannon wondered, or a tom?—was looking down, seeking a camping place, for windsteeds would not fly in darkness. Two midmen soared behind on smaller white mounts, pink-winged in the after-glow of the great sun Fomalhaut.

"Look there, Starlord!"

Rocannon's steed checked and snarled, seeing what Mogien was pointing to: a little black object moving low across the sky ahead of them, dragging behind it through the evening quiet a faint rattling noise. Rocannon gestured that they land at once. In the forest glade where they alighted, Mogien asked, "Was that a ship like yours, Starlord?"

"No. It was a planet-bound ship, a helicopter. It could only have been brought here on a ship much larger than mine was, a starfrigate or a transport. They must be coming here in force. And they must have started out before I did. What are they doing here anyhow, with bombers and helicopters? . . . They could shoot us right out of the sky from a long way off. We'll have to watch out for them, Lord Mogien."

"The thing was flying up from the Clayfields. I hope they were not there before us."

Rocannon only nodded, heavy with anger at the sight of that black spot on the sunset, that roach on a clean world. Whoever these people were that had bombed an unarmed Survey ship at sight, they evidently meant to survey this planet and take it over for colonization or for some military use. The High-Intelligence Life Forms of the planet, of which there were at least three species, all of low technological achievement, they would ignore or enslave or extirpate, whichever was most convenient. For to an aggressive people only technology mattered.

And there, Rocannon said to himself as he watched the midmen unsaddle the windsteeds and loose them for their night's hunting, right there perhaps was the League's own weak spot. Only technology mattered. The two missions to this world in the last century had started pushing one of the species toward a pre-atomic technology before they had even explored the other continents or contacted all intelligent races. He had called a halt to that, and had finally managed to bring his own Ethnographic Survey here to learn something about the planet; but he did not fool himself. Even his work here would finally have served only as an informational basis for encouraging technological advance in the most likely species or culture. This was how the League of All Worlds prepared to meet its ultimate enemy. A hundred worlds had been trained and armed, a thousand more were being schooled in the uses of steel and wheel and tractor and reactor. But Rocannon the hilfer, whose job was learning, not teaching, and who had lived on quite a few backward worlds, doubted the wisdom of staking everything on weapons and the uses of machines. Dominated by the aggressive, tool-making humanoid species of Centaurus, Earth, and the Cetians, the League had slighted certain skills and powers and potentialities of intelligent life, and judged by too narrow a standard.

This world, which did not even have a name yet beyond Formalhaut II, would probably never get much attention paid to it, for before the League's arrival none of its species seemed to have got beyond the lever and the forge. Other races on other worlds could be pushed ahead faster, to help when the extra-galactic enemy returned at last. No doubt this was inevitable. He thought of Mogien offering to fight a fleet of lightspeed bombers with the swords of Hallan. But what if lightspeed or even FTL bombers were very much like bronze swords, compared to the weapons of the Enemy? What if the weapons of the Enemy were things of the mind? Would it not be well to learn a little of the different shapes minds come in, and their powers? The League's policy was too narrow; it led to too much waste, and now evidently it had led to rebellion. If the storm brewing on Faraday ten years ago had broken, it meant that a young League world, having learned war promptly and been armed, was now out to carve its own empire from the stars.

He and Mogien and the two dark-haired servants gnawed hunks of good hard bread from the kitchens of Hallan, drank yellow *vaskan* from a skin flask, and soon settled to sleep. Very high all around their small fire stood the trees, dark branches laden with sharp, dark, closed cones. In the night a cold, fine rain whispered through the forest. Rocannon pulled the feathery herilo-fur bedroll up over his head and slept all the long night in the whisper of the rain. The windsteeds came back at daybreak, and before sunrise they were aloft again, windriding toward the pale lands near the gulf where the Clayfolk dwelt.

Landing about noon in a field of ray clay, Rocannon and the two servants, Raho and Yahan, looked about blankly, seeing no sign of life. Mogien said with the absolute confidence of his caste, "They'll come."

And they came: the squat hominoids Rocannon had seen in the museum years ago, six of them, not much taller than Rocannon's chest or Mogien's belt. They were naked, a whitish-gray color like their clay-fields, a singularly earthy-looking lot. When they spoke, they were uncanny, for there was no telling which one spoke; it seemed they all did, but with one harsh voice. *Partial colonial telepathy,* Rocannon recalled from the *Handbook,* and looked with increased respect at the ugly little men with their rare gift. His three tall companions evinced no such feeling. They looked grim.

"What do the Angyar and the servants of the Angyar wish in the field of the Lords of Night?" one of the Claymen, or all of them, was or were asking in the Common Tongue, an Angyar dialect used by all species.

"I am the Lord of Hallan," said Mogien, looking gigantic. "With me stands Rokanan, master of stars and the ways between the night, servant of the League of All Worlds, guest and friend of the Kinfolk of Hallan. High honor is due him! Take us to those fit to parley with us. There are words to be spoken, for soon there will be snow in warmyear and winds blowing backward and trees growing upside down!" The way the Angyar talked was a real pleasure, Rocannon thought, though its tact was not what struck you.

The Claymen stood about in dubious silence. "Truly this is so?" they or one of them asked at last.

"Yes, and the sea will turn to wood, and stones will grow toes! Take us to your chiefs, who know what a Starlord is, and waste no time!"

More silence. Standing among the little troglodytes, Rocannon had an uneasy sense as of mothwings brushing past his ears. A decision was being reached.

"Come," said the Claymen aloud, and led off across the sticky field. They gathered hurriedly around a patch of earth, stooped, then stood aside, revealing a hole in the ground and a ladder sticking out of it: the entrance to the Domain of Night.

While the midmen waited aboveground with the steeds, Mogien and Rocannon climbed down the ladder into a cave-world of crossing, branching tunnels cut in the clay and lined with coarse cement, electric-lighted, smelling of sweat and stale food. Padding on flat gray feet behind them, the guards took them to a half-lit, round chamber like a bubble in a great rock stratum, and left them there alone.

They waited. They waited longer.

Why the devil had the first surveys picked these people to encourage for League membership? Rocannon had a perhaps unworthy explanation: those first surveys had been from cold Centaurus, and the explorers had dived rejoicing into the caves of the Gdemiar, escaping the blinding floods of light and heat from the great A-3 sun. To them, sensible people lived underground on a world like this. To Rocannon, the hot white sun and the bright nights of quadruple moonlight, the intense weather-changes and ceaseless winds, the rich air and light gravity that permitted so many air-borne species, were all not only compatible but enjoyable. But, he reminded himself, just by that he was less well qualified than the Centaurans to judge these cave-folk. They were certainly clever. They were also telepathic—a power much rarer and much less well understood than electricity—but the first surveys had not made anything of that. They had given the Gdemiar a generator and a lock-drive ship and some math and some pats on the back, and left them. What had the little men done since? He asked a question along this line of Mogien.

The young lord, who had certainly never seen anything but a candle or a resin-torch in his life, glanced without the least interest at the electric light-bulb over his head. "They have always been good at making things," he said, with his extraordinary, straightforward arrogance.

"Have they made new sorts of things lately?"

"We buy our steel swords from the Clayfolk; they had smiths who could work steel in my grandfather's time; but before that I don't know. My people have lived a long time with Clayfolk, suffering them to tunnel beneath our border-lands, trading them silver for their swords. They are said to be rich, but forays on them are tabu. Wars between two breeds are evil matters—as you know. Even when my grandfather Durhal sought his wife here, thinking they had stolen her, he would not break the tabu to force them to speak. They will neither lie nor speak truth if they can help it. We do not love them, and they do not love us; I think they remember old days before the tabu. They are not brave."

A mighty voice boomed out behind their backs: "Bow down before the presence of the Lords of Night!" Rocannon had his hand on his lasergun and Mogien both hands on his sword-hilts as they turned; but Rocannon immediately spotted the speaker set in the curving wall, and murmured to Mogien, "Don't answer."

"Speak, O strangers in the Caverns of the Nightlords!" The sheer blare of sound was intimidating, but Mogien stood there without a blink, his high-arching eyebrows indolently raised. Presently he said, "Now you've wind-ridden three days, Lord Rokanan, do you begin to see the pleasure of it?"

"Speak and you shall be heard!"

"I do. And the striped steed goes light as the west wind in warmyear," Rocannon said, quoting a compliment overheard at table in the Revelhall.

"He's of very good stock."

"Speak! You are heard!"

They discussed windsteed-breeding while the wall bellowed at them. Eventually two Claymen appeared in the tunnel. "Come," they said stolidly. They led the strangers through further mazes to a very neat little electric-train system, like a giant but effective toy, on which they rode several miles more at a good clip, leaving the clay tunnels for what appeared to be a limestone-cave area. The last station was at the mouth of a fiercely-lighted hall, at the far end of which three troglodytes stood waiting on a dais. At first, to Rocannon's shame as an ethnologist, they all looked alike. As Chinamen had to the Dutch, as Russians had to the Centaurans. . . . Then he picked out the individuality of the central Clayman, whose face was lined, white, and powerful under an iron crown.

"What does the Starlord seek in the Caverns of the Mighty?"

The formality of the Common Tongue suited Rocannon's need precisely as he answered, "I had hoped to come as a guest to these caverns, to learn the ways of the Nightlords and see the wonders of their making. I hope yet to do so. But ill doings are afoot and I come now in haste and need. I am an officer of the League of All Worlds. I ask you to bring me to the starship which you keep as a pledge of the League's confidence in you."

The three stared impassively. The dais put them on a level with Rocannon, seen thus on a level, their broad, ageless faces and rock-hard eyes were impressive. Then, grotesquely, the left-hand one spoke in Pidgin-Galactic: "No ship," he said.

"There is a ship."

After a minute the one repeated ambiguously, "No ship."

"Speak the Common Tongue. I ask your help. There is an enemy to the League on this world. It will be your world no longer if you admit that enemy."

"No ship," said the left-hand Clayman. The other two stood like stalagmites.

"Then must I tell the other Lords of the League that the Clayfolk have betrayed their trust, and are unworthy to fight in the War To Come?"

Silence.

"Trust is on both sides, or neither," the iron-crowned Clayman in the center said in the Common Tongue.

"Would I ask your help if I did not trust you? Will you do this at least for me: send the ship with a message to Kerguelen? No one need ride it and lose the years; it will go itself."

Silence again.

"No ship," said the left-hand one in his gravel voice.

"Come, Lord Mogien," said Rocannon, and turned his back on them.

"Those who betray the Starlords," said Mogien in his clear arrogant voice, "betray older pacts. You made our swords of old, Clayfolk. They have not got rusty." And he strode out beside Rocannon, following the stump gray guides who led them in silence back to the railway, and through the maze of dank, glaring corridors, and up at last into the light of day.

They windrode a few miles west to get clear of the Clayfolk's territory, and landed on the bank of a forest river to take counsel.

Mogien felt he had let his guest down; he was not used to being thwarted in his generosity, and his self-possession was a little shaken. "Cave-grubs," he said. "Cowardly vermin! They will never say straight out what they have done or will do. All the Small Folk are like that, even the Fiia. But the Fiia can be trusted. Do you think the Clayfolk gave the ship to the enemy?"

"How can we tell?"

"I know this: they would give it to no one unless they were paid its price twice over. Things, things—they think of nothing but heaping up things. What did the old one mean, trust must be on both sides?"

"I think he meant that his people feel that we—the League—betrayed them. First we encourage them, then suddenly for forty-five years we drop them, send them no messages, discourage their coming, tell them to look after themselves. And that was my doing, though they don't know it. Why should they do me a favor, after all? I doubt they've talked with the enemy yet. But it would make no difference if they did bargain away the ship. The enemy could do even less with it than I could have done." Rocannon stood looking down at the bright river, his shoulders stooped.

"Rokanan," said Mogien, for the first time speaking to him as to a kinsman, "near this forest live my cousins of Kyodor, a strong castle, thirty Angyar swordsmen and three villages of midmen. They will help us punish the Clayfolk for their insolence—"

"No." Rocannon spoke heavily. "Tell your people to keep an eye on the Clayfolk, yes; they might be bought over by this enemy. But there will be no tabus broken or wars fought on my account. There is no point to it. In times like this, Mogien, one man's fate is not important."

"If it is not," said Mogien, raising his dark face, "what is?"

"Lords," said the slender young midman Yahan, "someone's over there among the trees." He pointed across the river to a flicker of color among the dark conifers.

"Fiia!" said Mogien. "Look at the windsteeds." All four of the big beasts were looking across the river, ears pricked.

"Mogien Hallanlord walks the Fiia's ways in friendship!" Mogien's voice rang over the broad, shallow, clattering water, and presently in mixed light and shadow under the trees on the other shore a small figure appeared. It seemed to dance a little as spots of sunlight played over it making it flicker and change, hard to keep the eyes on. When it moved, Rocannon thought it was walking on the surface of the river, so lightly it came, not stirring the sunlit shallows. The striped windsteed rose and stalked softly on thick, hollow-boned legs to the water's edge. As the Fian waded out of the water the big beast bowed its head, and the Fian reached up and scratched the striped, furry ears. Then he came toward them.

"Hail Mogien Halla's heir, sunhaired, swordbearer!" The voice was thin and sweet as a child's, the figure short and light as a child's, but it was no child's face. "Hail Hallan-guest, Starlord, Wanderer!" Strange, large, light eyes turned for a moment full on Rocannon.

"The Fiia know all names and news," said Mogien, smiling; but the little Fian did not smile in response. Even to Rocannon, who had only briefly visited one village of the species with the Survey team, this was startling.

"O Starlord," said the sweet, shaking voice, "who rides the windships that come and kill?"

"Kill—your people?"

"All my village," the little man said. "I was with the flocks out on the hills. I mindheard my people call, and I came, and they were in the flames burning and crying out.

There were two ships with turning wings. They spat out fire. Now I am alone and must speak aloud. Where my people were in my mind there is only fire and silence. Why was this done, Lords?"

He looked from Rocannon to Mogien. Both were silent. He bent over like a man mortally hurt, crouching, and hid his face.

Mogien stood over him, his hands on the hilts of his swords, shaking with anger. "Now I swear vengeance on those who harmed the Fiia! Rokanan, how can this be? The Fiia have no swords, they have no riches, they have no enemy! Look, his people are all dead, those he speaks to without words, his tribesmen. No Fian lives alone. He will die alone. Why would they harm his people?"

"To make their power known," Rocannon said harshly. "Let us bring him to Hallan, Mogien."

The tall lord knelt down by the little crouching figure. "Fian, man's-friend, ride with me. I cannot speak in your mind as your kinsmen spoke, but airborne works are not all hollow."

In silence they mounted, the Fian riding the high saddle in front of Mogien like a child, and the four steeds rose up again on the air. A rainy south wind favored their flight, and late the next day under the beating of his steed's wing Rocannon saw the marble stairway up through the forest, the Chasmbridge across the green abyss, and the towers of Hallan in the long western light.

The people of the castle, blond lords and dark-haired servants, gathered around them in the flightcourt, full of the news of the burning of the castle nearest them to the east, Reohan, and the murder of all its people. Again it had been a couple of helicopters and a few men armed with laser-guns; the warriors and farmers of Reohan had been slaughtered without giving one stroke in return. The people of Hallan were half berserk with anger and defiance, into which came an element of awe when they saw the Fian riding with their young lord and heard why he was there. Many of them, dwellers in this northermost fortress of Angien, had never seen one of the Fiia before, but all knew them as the stuff of legends and the subject of a powerful tabu. An attack, however bloody, on one of their own castles fit into their warrior outlook; but an attack on the Fiia was desecration. Awe and rage worked together in them. Late that evening in his tower room Rocannon heard the tumult from the Revelhall below, where the Angyar of Hallan all were gathered swearing destruction and extinction to the enemy in a torrent of metaphor and a thunder of hyperbole. They were a boastful race, the Angyar: vengeful, overweening, obstinate, illiterate, and lacking any first-person forms for the verb "to be unable." There were no gods in their legends, only heroes.

Through their distant racket a near voice broke in, startling Rocannon so his hand jumped on the radio tuner. He had at last found the enemy's communication band. A voice rattled on, speaking a language Rocannon did not know. Luck would have been too good if the enemy had spoken Galactic; there were hundreds of thousands of languages among the Worlds of the League, let alone the recognized planets such as this one and the planets still unknown. The voice began reading a list of numbers, which Rocannon understood, for they were in Cetian, the language of a race whose mathematical attainments had led to the general use throughout the League of Cetian mathematics and therefore Cetian numerals. He listened with strained attention, but it was no good, a mere string of numbers.

The voice stopped suddenly, leaving only the hiss of static.

Rocannon looked across the room to the little Fian, who had asked to stay with him, and now sat cross-legged and silent on the floor near the casement window.

"That was the enemy, Kyo."

The Fian's face was very still.

"Kyo," said Rocannon—it was the custom to address a Fian by the Angyar name of his village, since individuals of the species perhaps did and perhaps did not have individual names—"Kyo, if you tried, could you mindhear the enemies?"

In the brief notes from his one visit to a Fian village Rocannon had commented that Species 1-B seldom answered direct questions directly; and he well remembered their smiling elusiveness. But Kyo, left desolate in the alien country of speech, answered what Rocannon asked him. "No, Lord," he said submissively.

"Can you mindhear others of your own kind, in other villages?"

"A little. If I lived among them, perhaps . . . Fiia go sometimes to live in other villages than their own. It is said even that once the Fiia and the Gdemiar mindspoke together as one people, but that was very long ago. It is said . . ." He stopped.

"Your people and the Clayfolk are indeed one race, though you follow very different ways now. What more, Kyo?"

"It is said that very long ago, in the south, in the high places, the gray places, lived those who mindspoke with all creatures. All thoughts they could hear, the Old Ones, the Most Ancient. . . . But we came down from the mountains, and lived in the valleys and the caves, and have forgotten the harder way."

Rocannon pondered a moment. There were no mountains on the continent south of Hallan. He rose to get his *Handbook for Galactic Area Eight,* with its maps, when the radio, still hissing on the same band, stopped him short. A voice was coming through, much fainter, remote, rising and falling on billows of static, but speaking in Galactic. "Number Six, come in. Number Six, come in. This is Foyer. Come in, Number Six." After endless repetitions and pauses it continued: "This is Friday. No, this is Friday. . . . This is Foyer; are you there, Number Six? The FTLs are due tomorrow and I want a full report on the Seven Six sidings and the nets. Leave the staggering plan to the Eastern Detachment. Are you getting me, Number Six? We are going to be in ansible communication with

Base tomorrow. Will you get me that information on the sidings at once. Seven Six sidings. Unnecessary—" A surge of starnoise swallowed the voice, and when it re-emerged it was audible only in snatches. Ten long minutes went by in static, silence, and snatches of speech, then a nearer voice cut in, speaking quickly in the unknown language used before. It went on and on; moveless, minute after minute, his hand still on the cover of his *Handbook,* Rocannon listened. As moveless, the Fian sat in the shadows across the room. A double pair of numbers was spoken, then repeated; the second time Rocannon caught the Cetian word for "degrees." He flipped his notebook open and scribbled the numbers down; then at last, though he still listened, he opened the *Handbook* to the maps of Fomalhaut II.

The numbers he had noted were 28° 28—121° 40. If they were coördinates of latitude and longitude . . . He brooded over the maps a while, setting the point of his pencil down a couple of times on blank open sea. Then, trying 121 West with 28 North, he came down just south of a range of mountains, halfway down the Southwest Continent. He sat gazing at the map. The radio voice had fallen silent.

"Starlord?"

"I think they told me where they are. Maybe. And they've got an ansible there." He looked up at Kyo unseeingly, then back at the map. "If they're down there—if I could get there and wreck their game, if I could get just one message out on their ansible to the League, if I could . . ."

Southwest Continent had been mapped only from the air, and nothing but the mountains and major rivers were sketched inside the coastlines: hundreds of kilometers of blank, of unknown. And a goal merely guessed at.

"But I can't just sit here," Rocannon said. He looked up again, and met the little man's clear, uncomprehending gaze.

He paced down the stone-floored room and back. The radio hissed and whispered.

There was one thing in his favor: the fact that the enemy would not be expecting him. They thought they had the planet all to themselves. But it was the only thing in his favor.

"I'd like to use their weapons against them," he said. "I think I'll try to find them. In the land to the south. . . . My people were killed by these strangers, like yours, Kyo. You and I are both alone, speaking a language not our own. I would rejoice in your companionship."

He hardly knew what moved him to the suggestion.

The shadow of a smile went across the Fian's face. He raised his hands, parallel and apart. Rushlight in sconces on the walls bowed and flickered and changed. "It was foretold that the Wanderer would choose companions," he said. "For a while."

"The Wanderer?" Rocannon asked, but this time the Fian did not answer.

III

The Lady of the Castle crossed the high hall slowly, skirts rustling over stone. Her dark skin was deepened with age to the black of an ikon; her fair hair was white. Still she kept the beauty of her lineage. Rocannon bowed and spoke a greeting in the fashion of her people: "Hail Hallanlady, Durhal's daughter, Haldre the Fair!"

"Hail Rokanan, my guest," she said, looking calmly down at him. Like most Angyar women and all Angyar men she was considerably taller than he. "Tell me why you go south." She continued to pace slowly across the hall, and Rocannon walked beside her. Around them was dark air and stone, dark tapestry hung on high walls, the cool light of morning from clerestory windows slanting across the black of rafters overhead.

"I go to find my enemy, Lady."

"And when you have found them?"

"I hope to enter their . . . their castle, and make use of their . . . message-sender, to tell the League they are here, on this world. They are hiding here, and there is very little chance of their being found: the worlds are thick as sand on the sea-beach. But they must be found. They have done harm here, and they would do much worse on other worlds."

Haldre nodded her head once. "Is it true you wish to go lightly, with few men?"

"Yes, Lady. It is a long way, and the sea must be crossed. And craft, not strength, is my only hope against their strength."

"You will need more than craft, Starlord," said the old woman. "Well, I'll send with you four loyal midmen, if that suffices you, and two windsteeds laden and six saddled, and a piece or two of silver in case barbarians in the foreign lands want payment for lodging you, and my son Mogien."

"Mogien will come with me? These are great gifts, Lady, but that is the greatest!"

She looked at him a minute with her clear, sad, inexorable gaze. "I am glad it pleases you, Starlord." She resumed her slow walking, and he beside her. "Mogien desires to go, for love of you and for adventure; and you, a great lord on a very perilous mission, desire his company. So I think it is surely his way to follow. But I tell you now, this morning in the Long Hall, so that you may remember and not fear my blame if you return: I do not think he will come back with you."

"But Lady, he is the heir of Hallan."

She went in silence a while, turned at the end of the room under a time-darkened tapestry of winged giants fighting fair-haired men, and finally spoke again. "Hallan will find others heirs." Her voice was calm and bitter cold. "You Starlords are among us again, bringing new ways and wars. Reohan is dust; how long will Hallan stand? The world itself has become a grain of sand on the shore of night. All things change now. But I am certain still of one thing: that there is darkness over my lineage. My mother, whom you knew, was lost in the forests in her madness; my father was killed in battle, my husband by treachery; and when I bore a son my spirit grieved amid my joy, foreseeing his life would be short. That is no grief to him; he is an Angya, he wears the double swords. But my part of the darkness is to rule a failing domain alone, to live and live and outlive them all. . . ."

She was silent again a minute. "You may need more treasure than I can give you, to buy your life or your way. Take this. To you I give it, Rokanan, not to Mogien. There is no darkness on it to you. Was it not yours once, in the city across the night? To us it has been only a burden and a shadow. Take it back, Starlord; use it for a ransom or a gift." She unclasped from her neck the gold and the great blue stone of the necklace that had cost her mother's life, and held it out in her hand to Rocannon. He took it, hearing almost with terror the soft, cold clash of the golden links, and lifted his eyes to Haldre. She faced him, very tall, her blue eyes dark in the dark clear air of the hall. "Now take my son with you, Starlord, and follow your way. May your enemy die without sons."

Torchlight and smoke and hurrying shadows in the castle flightcourt, voices of beasts and men, racket and confusion, all dropped away in a few wingbeats of the striped steed Rocannon rode. Behind them now Hallan lay, a faint spot of light on the dark sweep of the hills, and there was no sound but a rushing of air as the wide half-seen wings lifted and beat down. The east was pale behind them, and the Greatstar burned like a bright crystal, heralding the sun, but it was long before daybreak. Day and night and the twilights were stately and unhurried on this planet that took thirty hours to turn. And the pace of the seasons also was large; this was the dawn of the vernal equinox, and four hundred days of spring and summer lay ahead.

"They'll sing songs of us in the high castles," said Kyo, riding postillion behind Rocannon. "They'll sing how the Wanderer and his companions rode south across the sky in the darkness before the spring. . . ." He laughed a little. Beneath them the hills and rich plains of Angien unfolded like a landscape painted on gray silk, brightening little by little, at last glowing vivid with colors and shadows as the lordly sun rose behind them.

At noon they rested a couple of hours by the river whose southwest course they were following to the sea; at dusk they flew down to a little castle, on a hilltop like all Angyar castles, near a bend of the same river. There they were made welcome by the lord of the place and his household. Curiosity obviously itched in him at the sight of a Fian traveling by windsteed, along with the Lord of Hallan, four midmen, and one who spoke with a queer accent, dressed like a lord, but wore no swords and was white-faced like a midman. To be sure, there was more intermingling between the two castes, the Angyar and Olgyior, than most Angyar like to admit; there were light-skinned warriors, and gold-haired servants; but this "Wanderer" was altogether too anomalous. Wanting no further rumor of his presence on the planet, Rocannon said nothing, and their host dared ask no questions of the heir of Hallan; so if he ever found out who his strange guests had been, it was from minstrels singing the tale, years later.

The next day passed the same for the seven travelers, riding the wind above the lovely land. They spent that night in an Olgyior village by the river, and on the third day came over country new even to Mogien. The river, curving away to the south, lay in loops and oxbows, the hills ran out into long plains, and far ahead was a mirrored pale brightness in the sky. Late in the day they came to a castle set alone on a white bluff, beyond which lay a long reach of lagoons and gray sand, and the open sea.

Dismounting, stiff and tired and his head ringing from wind and motion, Rocannon thought it the sorriest Angyar stronghold he had yet seen: a cluster of huts like wet chickens bunched under the wings of a squat, seedy-looking fort. Midmen, pale and short-bodied, peered at them from the straggling lanes. "They look as if they'd bred with Clayfolk," said Mogien. "This is the gate, and the place is called Tolen, if the wind hasn't carried us astray. Ho! Lords of Tolen, the guest is at your gate!"

There was no sound within the castle.

"The gate of Tolen swings in the wind," said Kyo, and they saw that indeed the portal of bronze-bound wood sagged on its hinges, knocking in the cold sea-wind that blew up through the town. Mogien pushed it open with his swordpoint. Inside was darkness, a scuttering rustle of wings, and a dank smell.

"The Lords of Tolen did not wait for their guests," said Mogien. "Well, Yahan, talk to these ugly fellows and find us lodging for the night."

The young midman turned to speak to the townsfolk

who had gathered at the far end of the castle forecourt to stare. One of them got up the courage to hitch himself forward, bowing and going sideways like some seaweedy beach-creature, and spoke humbly to Yahan. Rocannon could partly follow the Olgyior dialect, and gathered that the old man was pleading that the village had no proper housing for *pedanar,* whatever they were. The tall midman Raho joined Yahan and spoke fiercely, but the old man only hitched and bowed and mumbled, till at last Mogien strode forward. He could not by the Angyar code speak to the serfs of a strange domain, but he unsheathed one of his swords and held it up shining in the cold sea turned and shuffled down into the darkening alleys of the village. The travelers followed, the furled wings of their steeds brushing the low reed roofs on both sides.

"Kyo, what are pedanar?"

The little man smiled.

"Yahan, what is that word, pedanar?"

The young midman, a goodnatured, candid fellow, looked uneasy. "Well, Lord, a pedan is . . . one who walks among men . . ."

Rocannon nodded, snapping up even this scrap. While he had been a student of the species instead of its ally, he had kept seeking for their religion; they seemed to have no creeds at all. Yet they were quite credulous. They took spells, curses, and strange powers as matter of fact, and their relation to nature was intensely animistic; but they had no gods. This word, at last, smelled of the supernatural. It did not occur to him at the time that the word had been applied to himself.

It took three of the sorry huts to lodge the seven of them, and the windsteeds, too big to fit any house of the village, had to be tied outside. The beast huddled together, ruffling their fur against the sharp sea-wind. Rocannon's striped steed scratched at the wall and complained in a mewing snarl till Kyo went out and scratched its ears. "Worse awaits him soon, poor beast," said Mogien, sitting beside Rocannon by the stove-pit that warmed the hut. "They hate water."

"You said at Hallan that they wouldn't fly over the sea, and these villagers surely have no ships that would carry them. How are we going to cross the channel?"

"Have you your picture of the land?" Mogien inquired. The Angyar had no maps, and Mogien was fascinated by the Geographic Survey's maps in the *Handbook*. Rocannon got the book out of the old leather pouch he had carried from world to world, and which contained the little equipment he had had with him in Hallan when the ship had been bombed—*Handbook* and notebooks, suit and gun, medical kit and radio, a Terran chass-set and a battered volume of Hainish poetry. At first he had kept the necklace with its sapphire in with this stuff, but last night, oppressed by the value of the thing, he had sewn the sapphire pendant up in a little bag of soft barilor-hide and strung the necklace around his own neck, under his shirt and cloak, so that it looked like an amulet and could not be lost unless his head was too.

Mogien followed with a long, hard forefinger the contours of the two Western Continents where they faced each other: the far south of Angien, with its two deep gulfs and a fat promontory between them reaching south; and across the channel, the northermost cape of the Southwest Continent, which Mogien called Fiern. "Here we are," Rocannon said, setting a fish vertebra from their supper on the tip of the promontory.

"And here, if these cringing fish-eating yokels speak truth, is a castle called Plenot." Mogien put a second vertebra a half-inch east of the first one, and admired it. "A tower looks very like that from above. When I get back to Hallan, I'll send out a hundred men on steeds to look down on the land, and from their pictures we'll carve in stone a great picture of all Angien. Now at Plenot there will be ships—probably the ships of this place, Tolen, as well as their own. There was a feud between these two poor lords, and that's why Tolen stands now full of wind and night. So the old man told Yahan."

"Will Plenot lend us ships?"

"Plenot will *lend* us nothing. The lord of Plenot is an Errant." This meant, in the complex code of relationships among Angyar domains, a lord banned by the rest, an outlaw, not bound by the rules of hospitality, reprisal, or restitution.

"He has only two windsteeds," said Mogien, unbuckling his swordbelt for the night. "And his castle, they say, is built of wood."

Next morning as they flew down the wind to that wooden castle a guard spotted them almost as they spotted the tower. The two steeds of the castle were soon aloft, circling the tower; presently they could make out little figures with bows leaning from window-slits. Clearly an Errant Lord expected no friends. Rocannon also realized now why Angyar castles were roofed over, making them cavernous and dark inside, but protecting them from an airborne enemy. Plenot was a little place, ruder even than Tolen, lacking a village of midmen, perched out on a spit of black boulders above the sea; but poor as it was, Mogien's confidence that six men could subdue it seemed excessive. Rocannon checked the thighstraps of his saddle, shifted his grip on the long air-combat lance Mogien had given him, and cursed his luck and himself. This was no place for an ethnologist of forty-three.

Mogien, flying well ahead on his black steed, raised his lance and yelled. Rocannon's mount put down its head and beat into full flight. The black-and-gray wings flashed up and down like vans; the long, thick, light body was tense, thrumming with the powerful heartbeat. As the wind whistled past, the thatched tower of Plenot seemed to hurtle toward them, circled by two rearing gryphons. Rocannon crouched down on the windsteed's back, his long lance couched ready. A happiness, an old delight was swelling in him; he laughed a little, riding the wind. Closer and closer came the rocking tower and its two winged guards, and suddenly with a piercing falsetto shout Mogien hurled his lance, a bolt of silver through the air. It hit one rider square in the chest, breaking his thighstraps with the force of the blow, and hurled him over his steed's haunches in a clear, seemingly slow arc three hundred feet down to the breakers creaming quietly on the rocks. Mogien shot straight on past the riderless steed and opened combat with the other guard, fighting in close, trying to get a sword-stroke past the lance which his opponent did not throw but used for jabbing and parrying. The four midmen on their white and gray mounts hovered nearby like terrible pigeons, ready to help but not interfering with their lord's duel, circling just high enough that the archers below could not pierce the steeds' leathern bellymail. But all at once all four of them, with that nerve-rending falsetto yell, closed in on the duel. For a moment there was a knot of white wings and glittering steel hanging in midair. From the knot dropped a figure that seemed to be trying to lie down on the air, turning this way and that with loose limbs seeking comfort, till it struck the castle roof and slid to a hard bed of rock below.

Now Rocannon saw why they had joined in the duel: the guard had broken its rules and struck at the steed instead of the rider. Mogien's mount, purple blood staining one black wing, was straining inland to the dunes. Ahead of him shot the midmen, chasing the two riderless steeds, which kept circling back, trying to get to their safe stables in the castle. Rocannon headed them off, driving his steed right at them over the castle roofs. He saw Raho catch one with a long cast of his rope, and at the same moment felt something sting his leg. His jump startled his excited steed; he reined in too hard, and the steed arched up its back and for the first time since he had ridden it began to buck, dancing and prancing all over the wind above the castle. Arrows played around him like reversed rain. The midmen and Mogien mounted on a wild-eyed yellow steed shot past him, yelling and laughing. His mount straightened out and followed them. "Catch, Starlord!" Yahan yelled, and a comet with a black tail came arching at him. He caught it in self-defense, found it is lighted resin-torch, and joined the others in circling the tower at close range, trying to set its thatch roof and wooden beams alight.

"You've got an arrow in your left leg," Mogien called as he passed Rocannon, who laughed hilariously and hurled his torch straight into a window-slit from which an archer leaned. "Good shot!" cried Mogien, and came plummeting down onto the tower roof, re-arising from it in a rush of flame.

Yahan and Raho were back with more sheaves of smoking torches they had set alight on the dunes, and were dropping these wherever they saw reed or wood to set afire. The tower was going up now in a roaring fountain of sparks, and the windsteeds, infuriated by constant reining in and by the sparks stinging their coats, kept plunging down toward the roofs of the castle, making a coughing roar very horrible to hear. The upward rain of arrows had ceased, and now a man scurried out into the forecourt, wearing what looked like a wooden salad bowl on his head, and holding up in his hands what Rocannon first took for a mirror, then saw was a bowl full of water. Jerking at the reins of the yellow beast, which was still trying to get back down to its stable, Mogien rode over the man and called, "Speak quick! My men are lighting new torches!"

"Of what domain, Lord?"

"Hallan!"

"The Lord-Errant of Plenot craves time to put out the fires, Hallanlord!"

"In return for the lives and treasures of the men of Tolen, I grant it."

"So be it," cried the man, and, still holding up the full bowl of water, he trotted back into the castle. The attackers withdrew to the dunes and watched the Plenot folk rush out to man their pump and set up a bucket-brigade from the sea. The tower burned out, but they kept the walls and hall standing. There were only a couple of dozen of them, counting some women. When the fires were out, a group of them came on foot from the gate, over the rocky spit and up the dunes. In front walked a tall, thin man with the walnut skin and fiery hair of the Angyar; behind him came two soldiers still wearing their salad-bowl helmets, and behind them six ragged men and women staring about sheepishly. The tall man raised in his two hands the clay bowl filled with water. "I am Ogoren of Plenot, Lord-Errant of this domain."

"I am Mogien Halla's heir."

"The lives of the Tolenfolk are yours, Lord." He nodded to the ragged group behind him. "No treasure was in Tolen."

"There were two longships, Errant."

"From the north the dragon flies, seeing all things," Ogoren said rather sourly. "The ships of Tolen are yours."

"And you will have your windsteeds back, when the ships are at Tolen wharf," said Mogien, magnanimous.

"By what other lord had I the honor to be defeated?" Ogoren asked with a glance at Rocannon, who wore all the gear and bronze armor of an Angyar warrior, but no swords. Mogien too looked at his friend, and Rocannon responded with the first alias that came to mind, the name Kyo called him by—"Olhor," the Wanderer.

Ogoren gazed at him curiously, then bowed to both and said, "The bowl is full, Lords."

"Let the water not be spilled and the pact not be broken!"

Ogoren turned and strode with his two men back to his smouldering fort, not giving a glance to the freed prisoners huddled on the dune. To these Mogien said only, "Lead home my windsteed; his wing was hurt," and, remounting the yellow beast from Plenot, he took off. Rocannon followed, looking back at the sad little group as they began their trudge home to their own ruinous domain.

By the time he reached Tolen his battle-spirits had flagged and he was cursing himself again. There had in fact been an arrow sticking out of his left calf when he'd dismounted on the dun, painless till he had pulled it out without stopping to see if the point were barbed, which it was. The Angyar certainly did not use poison; but there was always blood poisoning. Swayed by his companions' genuine courage, he had been ashamed to wear his protective and almost invisible impermasuit for this foray. Owning armor that could withstand a laser-gun, he might die in this damned hovel from the scratch of a bronze-headed arrow. And he had set off to save a planet, when he could not even save his own skin.

The oldest midman from Hallan, a quiet stocky fellow named Iot, came in and almost wordlessly, gentle-mannered, knelt and washed and bandaged Rocannon's hurt. Mogien followed, still in battle dress, looking ten feet tall with his crested helmet and five feet across the shoulders exaggerated by the stiff winglike shoulderboard of his cape. Behind him came Kyo, silent as a child among the warriors of a stronger face. Then Yahan came in, and Raho, and young Bien, so that the hut creaked at the seams when they all squatted around the stove-pit. Yahan filled seven silver-bound cups, which Mogien gravely passed around. They drank. Rocannon began to feel better. Mogien inquired of his wound, and Rocannon felt much better. They drank more vaskan, while scared and admiring faces of villagers peered momentarily in the doorway from the twilit lane outside. Rocannon felt benevolent and heroic. They ate, and drank more, and then in the airless hut reeking with smoke and fried fish and harness-grease and sweat, Yahan stood up with a lyre of bronze with silver strings, and sang. He sang of Durholde of Hallan who set free the prisoners of Korhalt, in the days of the Red Lord, by the marshes of Born; and when he had sung the lineage of every warrior in that battle and every stroke he struck, he sang straight on the freeing of the Tolenfolk and the burning of Plenot Tower, of the Wanderer's torch blazing through a rain of arrows, of the great stroke struck by Mogien Halla's heir, the lance cast across the wind finding its mark like the unerring lance of Hendin in the days of old. Rocannon sat drunk and contented, riding the river of song, feeling himself now wholly committed, sealed by his shed blood to this world to which he had come a stranger across the gulfs of night. Only beside him now and then he sensed the presence of the little Fian, smiling, alien, serene.

IV

THE SEA STRETCHED in long misty swells under a smoking rain. No color was left in the world. Two windsteeds, wing-bound and chained in the stern of the boat, lamented and yowled, and over the swells through rain and mist came a doleful echo from the other boat.

They had spent many days at Tolen, waiting till Rocannon' leg healed, and till the black windsteed could fly again. Though these were reasons to wait, the truth was that Mogien was reluctant to leave, to cross the sea they must cross. He roamed the gray sands among the lagoons below Tolen all alone, struggling perhaps with the premonition that had visited his mother Haldre. All he could say to Rocannon was that the sound and sight of the sea made his heart heavy. When at last the black steed was fully cured, he abruptly decided to send it back to Hallan in Bien's care, as if saving one valuable thing from peril. They had also agreed to leave the two packsteeds and most of their load to the old Lord of Tolen and his nephews, who were still creeping about trying to patch their drafty castle. So now in the two dragon-headed boats on the rainy sea were only six travelers and five steeds, all of them wet and most of them complaining.

Two morose fishermen of Tolen sailed the boat. Yahan was trying to comfort the chained steeds with a long and monotonous lament for a long-dead lord; Rocannon and the Fian, cloaked and with hoods pulled over their heads, were in the bow. "Kyo, once you spoke of mountains to the south."

"Oh yes," said the little man, looking quickly northward, at the lost coast of Angien.

"Do you know anything of the people that live in the southern land—in Fiern?"

His *Handbook* was not much help; after all, it was to fill the vast gaps in the *Handbook* that he had brought his Survey here. It postulated five High-Intelligence Life Forms for the planet, but described only three: the Angyar/Olgyior; the Fiia and Gdemiar; and a non-humanoid species found on the great Eastern Continent on the other side of the planet. The geographers' notes on Southwest Continent were mere hearsay: *Unconfirmed species ?4: Large humanoids said to inhabit extensive towns* (?). *Unconfirmed Species ?5: Winged marsupials.* All in all, it was about as helpful as Kyo, who often seemed to believe that Rocannon knew the answers to all the questions he asked, and now replied like a schoolchild, "In Fiern live the Old Races, is it not so?" Rocannon had to content himself with gazing southward into the mist that hid the questionable land, while the great bound beasts howled and the rain crept chilly down his neck.

Once during the crossing he thought he heard the racket of a helicopter overhead, and was glad the fog hid them; then he shrugged. Why hide? The army using this planet as their base for interstellar warfare were not going to be very badly scared by the sight of ten men and five overgrown housecats bobbing in the rain in a pair of leaky boats. . . .

They sailed on in a changeless circle of rain and waves. Misty darkness rose from the water. A long, cold night went by. Gray light grew, showing mist, and rain, and waves. Then suddenly the two glum sailors in each boat came alive, steering and staring anxiously ahead. A cliff loomed all at once above the boats, fragmentary in the writhing fog. As they skirted its base, boulders and wind-dwarfed trees hung high over their sails.

Yahan had been questioning one of the sailors. "He says we'll sail past the mouth of a big river here, and on the other side is the only landingplace for a long way." Even as he spoke the overhanging rocks dropped back into mist and a thicker fog swirled over the boat, which creaked as a new current struck her keel. The grinning dragon head at the bow rocked and turned. The air was white and opaque; the water breaking and boiling at the sides was opaque and red. The sailors yelled to each other and to the other boat. "The river's in flood," Yahan said. "They're trying to turn— Hang on!" Rocannon caught Kyo's arm as the boat yawed and then pitched and spun on crosscurrents, doing a kind of crazy dance while the sailors fought to hold her steady, and blind mist hid the water, and the windsteeds struggled to free their wings, snarling with terror.

The dragonhead seemed to be going forward steady again, when in a gust of fog-laden wind the unhandy boat jibbed and heeled over. The sail hit water with a slap, caught as if in glue, and pulled the boat right over on her side. Red, warm water quietly came up to Rocannon's face, filled his mouth, filled his eyes. He held on to whatever he was holding and struggled to find the air again. It was Kyo's arm he had hold of, and the two of them floundered in the wild sea warm as blood that swung them and rolled them and tugged them farther from the capsized boat. Rocannon yelled for help, and his voice fell dead in the blank silence of fog over the waters. Was there a shore— which way, how far? He swam after the dimming hulk of the boat, Kyo dragging on his arm.

"Rokanan!"

The dragonhead prow of the other boat loomed grinning out of the white chaos. Mogien was overboard, fighting the current beside him, getting a rope into his hands and around Kyo's chest. Rocannon saw Mogien's face vividly, the arched eyebrows and yellow hair dark with water. They were hauled up into the boat, Mogien last.

Yahan and one of the fishermen from Tolen had been picked up right away. The other sailor and the two windsteeds were drowned, caught under the boat. They were far enough out in the bay now that the flood-currents and winds from the river-gorge were weaker. Crowded with soaked, silent men, the boat rocked on through the red water and the wreathing fog.

"Rokanan, how comes it you're not wet?"

Still dazed, Rocannon looked down at his sodden clothing and did not understand. Kyo, smiling, shaking with cold, answered for him: "The Wanderer wears a second skin." of his impermasuit, which he had put on for warmth in the damp cold last night, leaving only head and hands bare. So he still had it, and the Eye of the Sea still lay hidden on his breast; but his radio, his maps, his gun, all other links with his own civilization, were gone.

"Yahan, you will go back to Hallan."

The servant and his master stood face to face on the shore of the southern land, in the fog, surf hissing at their feet. Yahan did not reply.

They were six riders now, with three windsteeds. Kyo could ride with one midman and Rocannon with another, but Mogien was too heavy a man to ride double for long distances; to spare the windsteeds, the third midman must go back with the boat to Tolen. Mogien had decided Yahan, the youngest, should go.

"I do not send you back for anything ill done or undone, Yahan. Now go—the sailors are waiting."

The servant did not move. Behind him the sailors were kicking apart the fire they had eaten by. Pale sparks flew up briefly in the fog.

"Lord Mogien," Yahan whispered, "send Iot back."

Mogien's face got dark, and he put a hand on his sword-hilt.

"Go, Yahan!"

"I will not go, Lord."

The sword came hissing out of its sheath, and Yahan with a cry of despair dodged backward, turned, and disappeared into the fog.

"Wait for him a while," Mogien said to the sailors, his face impassive. "Then go on your way. We must seek our way now. Small Lord, will you ride my steed while he walks?" Kyo sat huddled up as if very cold; he had not eaten, and had not spoken a word since they landed on the coast of Fiern. Mogien set him on the gray steed's saddle and walked at the beast's head, leading them up the beach away from the sea. Rocannon followed, glancing back after Yahan and ahead at Mogien, wondering at the strange being, his friend, who one moment would have killed a man in cold wrath and the next moment spoke with simple kindness. Arrogant and loyal, ruthless and kind, in his very disharmony Mogien was lordly.

The fisherman had said there was a settlement east of this cove, so they went east now in the pallid fog that surrounded them in a soft dome of blindness. On windsteeds they might have got above the fog-blanket, but the big animals, worn out and sullen after being tied two days in the boat, would not fly. Mogien, Iot and Raho led them, and Rocannon followed behind, keeping a surreptitious lookout for Yahan, of whom he was fond. He had kept on his impermasuit for warmth, though not the headpiece, which insulated him entirely from the world. Even so, he felt uneasy in the blind mist walking an unknown shore, and he searched the sand as he went for any kind of staff or stick. Between the grooves of the windsteeds' dragging wings and ribbons of seaweed and dried salt scum he saw a long white stick of driftwood; he worked it free of the sand and felt easier, armed. But by stopping he had fallen far behind. He hurried after companions' tracks through the fog. A figure loomed up to his right. He knew at once it was none of his companions, and brought his stick up like a quarterstaff, but was grabbed from behind and pulled down backwards. Something like wet leather was slapped across his mouth. He wrestled free and was rewarded with a blow on his head that drove him into unconsciousness.

When sensation returned, painfully and a little at a time, he was lying on his back in the sand. High up above him two vast foggy figures were ponderously arguing. He understood only part of their Olgyior dialect. "Leave it here," one said, and the other said something like, "Kill it here, it hasn't got anything." At this Rocannon rolled on his side and pulled the headmask of his suit up over his head and face and sealed it. One of the giants turned to peer down at him and he saw it was only a burly midman bundled in furs. "Take it to Zgama, maybe Zgama wants it," the other one said. After more discussion Rocannon was hauled up by the arms and dragged along at a jogging run. He struggled, but his head swam and the fog had got into his brain. He had some consciousness of the mist growing darker, of voices, of a wall of sticks and clay and interwoven reeds, and a torch flaring in a sconce. Then a roof overhead, and more voices, and the dark. And finally, face down on a stone floor, he came to and raised his head.

Near him a long fire blazed in a hearth the size of a hut. Bare legs and hems of ragged pelts made a fence in front of it. He raised his head farther and saw a man's face: a midman, white-skinned, black-haired, heavily bearded, clothed in green and black striped furs, a square fur hat on his head. "What are you?" he demanded in a harsh bass, glaring down at Rocannon.

"I . . . I ask the hospitality of this hall," Rocannon said when he had got himself onto his knees. He could not at the moment get any farther.

"You've had some of it," said the bearded man, watching him feel the lump on his occiput. "Want more?" The muddy legs and fur rags around him jigged, dark eyes peered, white faces grinned.

Rocannon got to his feet and straightened up. He stood silent and motionless till his balance was steady and the hammering of pain in his skull had lessened. Then he lifted his head and gazed into the bright black eyes of his captor. "You are Zgama," he said.

The bearded man stepped backwards, looking scared. Rocannon, who had been in trying situations on several worlds, followed up his advantage as well as he could. "I am Olhor, the Wanderer. I come from the north and from the sea, from the land behind the sun. I come in peace and I go in peace. Passing by the Hall of Zgama, I go south. Let no man stop me!"

"Ahh," said all the open mouths in the white faces, gazing at him. He kept his own eyes unwavering Zgama.

"I am master here," the big man said, his voice rough and uneasy. "None pass by me!"

Rocannon did not speak, or blink.

Zgama saw that in this battle of eyes he was losing: all his people still gazed with round eyes at the stranger. "Leave off your staring!" he bellowed. Rocannon did not move. He realized he was up against a defiant nature, but it was too late to change his tactics now. "Stop staring!" Zgama roared again, then whipped a sword from under his fur cloak, whirled it, and with a tremendous blow sheered off the stranger's head.

But the stranger's head did not come off. He staggered, but Zgama's swordstroke had rebounded as from rock. All the people around the fire whispered, "Ahhh!" The stranger steadied himself and stood unmoving, his eyes fixed on Zgama.

Zgama wavered; almost he stood back to let this weird prisoner go. But the obstinacy of his race won out over his bafflement and fear. "Catch him—grab his arms!" he roared, and when his men did not move he grabbed Rocannon's shoulders and spun him around. At that his men moved in, and Rocannon made no resistace. His suit protected him from foreign elements, extreme temperatures, radioactivity, shocks, and blows of moderate velocity and weight such as swordstrokes or bullets; but it could not get him out of the grasp of ten or fifteen strong men.

"No man passes by the Hall of Zgama, Master of the Long Bay!" The big man gave his rage full vent when his braver bullies had got Rocannon pinioned. "You're a spy for the Yellowheads of Angien. I know you! You come with your Angyar talk and spells and tricks, and dragonboats will follow you out of the north. Not to this place! I am the master of the masterless. Let the Yellowheads and their lickspittle slaves come here—we'll give 'em a taste of bronze! You crawl up out of the sea asking a place by my fire, do you? I'll get you warm, spy. I'll give you roast meat, spy. Tie him to the post there!" His brutal bluster had heartened his people, and they jostled to help lash the stranger to one of the hearth-posts that supported a great spit over the fire, and to pile up wood around his legs.

Then they fell silent. Zgama strode up, grim and massive in his furs, took up a burning branch from the hearth and shook it in Rocannon's eyes, then set the pyre aflame. It blazed up hot. In a moment Rocannon's clothing, the brown cloak and tunic of Hallan, took fire and flamed up around his head, at his face.

"Ahhh," all the watchers whispered once more, but one of them cried, "Look!" As the blaze died down they saw through the smoke the figure stand motionless, flames licking up its legs, gazing straight at Zgama. On the naked breast, dropping from a chain of gold, shone a great jewel like an open eye.

"Pedan, pedan," whimpered the women, cowering in dark corners.

Zgama broke the hush of panic with his bellowing voice. "He'll burn! Let him burn! Deho, throw on more wood, the spy's not roasting quick enough!" He dragged a little boy out into the leaping, restless firelight and forced him to add wood to the pyre. "Is there nothing to eat? Get food, you women! You see our hospitality, you Olhor, see how we eat?" He grabbed a joint of meat off the trencher a woman offered him, and stood in front of Rocannon tearing at it and letting the juice run down his beard. A couple of his bullies imitated him, keeping a little farther away. Most of them did not come anywhere near that end of the hearth; but Zgama got them to eat and drink and shout, and some of the boys dared one another to come up close enough to add a stick to the pyre where the mute, calm man stood with flames playing along his red-lit, strangly shining skin.

Fire and noise died down at last. Men and women slept curled up in their fur rags on the floor, in corners, in the warm ashes. A couple of men watched, sword on knees and flask in hand.

Rocannon let his eyes close. By crossing two fingers he unsealed the headzone of his suit, and breathed fresh air again. The long night wore along and slowly the long dawn lightened. In gray daylight, through fog wreathing in the windowholes, Zgama came sliding on greasy spots on the floor and stepping over snoring bodies, and peered at his captive. The captive's gaze was grave and steady, the captor's impotently defiant. "Burn, burn!" Zgama growled, and went off.

Outside the rude hall Rocannon heard the cooing mutter of herilor, the fat and feathery domesticated meat-animals of the Angyar, kept wing-clipped and here pastured probably on the sea-cliffs. The hall emptied out except for a few babies and women, who kept well away from him even when it came time to roast the evening meat.

By then Rocannon had stood bound for thirty hours, and was suffering both pain and thirst. That was his deadline, thirst. He could go without eating for a long time, and supposed he could stand in chains at least as long, though his head was already light; but without water he could get through only one more of these long days.

Powerless as he was, there was nothing he could say to Zgama, threat or bribe, that would not simply increase the barbarian's obduracy.

That night as the fire danced in front of his eyes and through it he watched Zgama's bearded, heavy, white face, he kept seeing in his mind's eye a different face, bright-haired and dark: Mogien, whom he had come to love as a friend and somewhat as a son. As the night and the fire went on and on he thought also of the little Fian Kyo, childlike and uncanny, bound to him in a way he had not tried to understand; he saw Yahan singing of heroes; and Iot and Raho grumbling and laughing together as they curried the great-winged steeds; and Haldre unclasping the gold chain from her neck. Nothing came to him from all his earlier life, though he had lived many years on many worlds, learned much, done much. It was all burnt away. He thought he stood in Hallan, in the long hall hung with tapestries of men fighting giants, and that Yahan was offering him a bowl of water.

"Drink it, Starlord. Drink."

And he drank.

V

FENI AND FELI, the two largest moons, danced in white reflections on the water as Yahan held a second bowlful for him to drink. The hearthfire glimmered only in a few coals. The hall was dark picked out with flecks and shafts of moonlight, silent except for the breathing and shifting of many sleepers.

As Yahan cautiously loosed the chains Rocannon leaned his full weight back against the post, for his legs were numb and he could not stand unsupported.

"They guard the outer gate all night," Yahan was whispering in his ear, "and those guards keep awake. Tomorrow when they take the flocks out—"

"Tomorrow night. I can't run. I'll have to bluff out. Hook the chain so I can lean my weight on it, Yahan. Get the hook here, by my hand." A sleeper nearby sat up pawning, and with a grin that flashed a moment in the moonlight Yahan sank down and seemed to melt in shadows.

Rocannon saw him at dawn going out with the other men to take the herilor to pasture, wearing a muddy pelt like the others, his black hair sticking out like a broom. Once again Zgama came up and scowled at his captive. Rocannon knew the man would have given half his flocks and wives to be rid of his unearthly guest, but was trapped in his own cruelty: the jailer is the prisoner's prisoner. Zgama had slept in the warm ashes and his hair was smeared with ash, so that he looked more the burned man than Rocannon, whose naked skin shone white. He stamped off, and again the hall was empty most of the day, though guards stayed at the door. Rocannon improved his time with surreptitious isometric exercises. When a passing woman caught him stretching, he stretched on, swaying and emitting a low, weird croon. She dropped to all fours and scuttled out, whimpering.

Twilit fog blew in the windows, sullen womenfolk boiled a stew of meat and seaweed, returning flocks cooed in hundreds outside, and Zgama and his men came in, fog-droplets glittering in their beards and furs. They sat on the floor to eat. The place rang and reeked and steamed. The strain of returning each night to the uncanny was showing; faces were grim, voices quarrelsome. "Build up the fire—he'll roast yet!" shouted Zgama, jumping up to push a burning log over onto the pyre. None of his men moved.

"I'll eat your heart, Olhor, when it fries out between your ribs! I'll wear that blue stone for a nosering!" Zgama was shaking with rage, frenzied by the silent steady gaze he had endured for two nights. "I'll make you shut your eyes!" he screamed, and snatching up a heavy stick from the floor he brought it down with a whistling crack on Rocannon's head, jumping back at the same moment as if afraid of what he handled. The stick fell among the burning logs and stuck up at an angle.

Slowly, Rocannon reached out his right hand, closed his fist about the stick and drew it out of the fire. Its end was ablaze. He raised it till it pointed at Zgama's eyes, and then, as slowly, he stepped forward. The chains fell away from him. The fire leaped up and broke apart in sparks and coals about his bare feet.

"Out!" he said, coming straight at Zgama, who fell back one step and then another. "You're not master here. The lawless man is a slave, and the cruel man is a slave, and the stupid man is a slave. You are my slave, and I drive you like a beast. Out!" Zgama caught both sides of the doorframe, but the blazing staff came at his eyes, and he cringed back into the courtyard. The guards crouched down, motionless. Resin-torches flaring beside the outer gate brightened the fog; there was no noise but the murmur of the herds in their byres and the hissing of the sea below the cliffs. Step by step Zgama went backward till he reached the outer gate between the torches. His black- and-white face stared masklike as the fiery staff came closer. Dumb with fear, he clung to the log doorpost, filling the gateway with his bulky body. Rocannon, exhausted and vindictive, drove the flaming point hard against his chest, pushed him down, and strode over his body into the blackness and blowing fog outside the gate. He went about fifty paces into the dark, then stumbled, and could not get up.

No one pursued. No one came out of the compound behind him. He lay half-conscious in the dune-grass. After a long time the gate torches died out or were extinguished, and there was only darkness. Wind blew with voices in the grass, and the sea hissed down below.

As the fog thinned, letting the moons shine through, Yahan found him there near the cliff's edge. With his help, Rocannon got up and walked. Feeling their way, stumbling, crawling on hands and knees where the going was rough and dark, they worked eastward and southward away from the coast. A couple of times they stopped to get their breath and bearings, and Rocannon fell asleep almost as soon as they stopped. Yahan woke him and kept him going until, some time before dawn, they came down a valley under the eaves of a steep forest. The domain of trees was black in the misty dark. Yahan and Rocannon entered it along the streambed they had been following, but did not go far. Rocannon stopped and said in his own language, "I can't go any farther." Yahan found a sandy strip under the streambank where they could lie hidden at least from above; Rocannon crawled into it like an animal into its den, and slept.

When he woke fifteen hours later at dusk, Yahan was there with a small collection of green shoots and roots to eat. "It's too early in warmyear for fruit," he explained ruefully, "and the oafs in Oafscastle took my bow. I made some snares but they won't catch anything till tonight."

Rocannon consumed the salad avidly, and when he had drunk from the stream and stretched and could think again, he asked, "Yahan, how did you happen to be there—in Oafscastle?"

The young midman looked down and buried a few inedible root-tips neatly in the sand. "Well, Lord, you know that I . . . defied my Lord Mogien. So after that, I thought I might join the Masterless."

"You'd heard of them before?"

"There are tales at home of places where we Olgyior are both lords and servants. It's even said that in old days only we midmen lived in Angien, and were hunters in the forests and had no masters; and the Angyar came from the south in dragonboats. . . . Well, I found the fort, and Zgama's fellows took me for a runaway from some other place down the coast. They grabbed my bow and put me to work and asked no questions. So I found you. Even if you hadn't been there I would have escaped. I would not be a lord among such oafs!"

"Do you know where our companions are?"

"No. Will you seek for them, Lord?"

"Call me by my name, Yahan. Yes, if there's any chance of finding them I'll seek them. We can't cross a continent alone, on foot, without clothes or weapons."

Yahan said nothing, smoothing the sand, watching the stream that ran dark and clear beneath the heavy branches of the conifers.

"You disagree?"

"If my Lord Mogien finds me he'll kill me. It is his right."

By the Angyar code, this was true; and if anyone would keep the code, it was Mogien.

"If you find a new master, the old one may not touch you: is that not true, Yahan?"

The boy nodded. "But a rebellious man finds no new master."

"That depends. Pledge your service to me, and I'll answer for you to Mogien—if we find him. I don't know what words you use."

"We say"—Yahan spoke very low—*"to my Lord I give the hours of my life and the use of my death."*

"I accept them. And with them my own life which you gave back to me."

The little river ran noisily from the ridge above them, and the sky darkened solemnly. In late dusk Rocannon slipped off his impermasuit and, stretching out in the stream, let the cold water running all along his body wash away sweat and weariness and fear and the memory of the fire licking at his eyes. Off, the suit was a handful of transparent stuff and semivisible, hairthin tubes and wires and a couple of translucent cubes the size of a fingernail. Yahan watched him with an uncomfortable look as he put the suit on again (since he had no clothes, and Yahan had been forced to trade his Angyar clothing for a couple of dirty herilo fleeces). "Lord Olhor," he said at last, "it was . . . was it that skin that kept the fire from burning you? Or the . . . the jewel?"

The necklace was hidden now in Yahan's own amulet-bag, around Rocannon's neck. Rocannon answered gently, "The skin. No spells. It's a very strong kind of armor."

"And the white staff?"

He looked down at the driftwood stick, one end of it heavily charred; Yahan had picked it up from the grass of the sea-cliff, last night, just as Zgama's men had brought it along to the fort with him; they had seemed determined he should keep it. What was a wizard without his staff? "Well," he said, "it's a good walking-stick, if we've got to walk." He stretched again, and for want of more supper before they slept, drank once more from the dark, cold, noisy stream.

Late next morning when he woke, he was recovered, and ravenous. Yahan had gone off at dawn, to check his snares and because he was too cold to lie longer in their damp den. He returned with only a handful of herbs, and a piece of bad news. He had crossed over the forested ridge which they were on the seaward side of, and from its top had seen to the south another broad reach of the sea.

"Did those misbegotten fish-eaters from Tolen leave us on an island?" he growled, his usual optimism subverted by cold, hunger, and doubt.

Rocannon tried to recall the coastline on his drowned maps. A river running in from the west emptied on the north of a long tongue of land, itself part of a coastwise mountainchain running west to east; between that tongue and the mainland was a sound, long and wide enough to show up very clear on the maps and in his memory. A hundred, two hundred kilometers long? "How wide?" he asked Yahan, who answered glumly, "Very wide. I can't swim, Lord."

"We can walk. This ridge joins the mainland, west of here. Mogien will be looking for us along that way, probably." It was up to him to provide leadership—Yahan had certainly done more than his share—but his heart was low in him at the thought of that long detour through unknown and hostile country. Yahan had seen no one, but had crossed paths, and there must be men in these woods to make the game so scarce and shy.

But for there to be any hope of Mogien's find them—if Mogien was alive, and free, and still had the windsteeds—they would have to work southward, and if possible out into open country. He would look for them going south, for that was all the goal of their journey. "Let's go," Rocannon said, and they went.

A little after midday they looked down from the ridge across a broad inlet running east and west as far as eye could see, lead-gray under a low sky. Nothing of the southern shore could be made out but a line of low, dark, dim hills. The wind that blew up the sound was bitter cold at their backs as they worked down to the shore and started westward along it. Yahan looked up at the clouds, hunched his head down between his shoulders and said mournfully, "It's going to snow."

And presently the snow began, a wet windblown snow of spring, vanishing on the wet ground as quickly as on the dark water of the sound. Rocannon's suit kept the cold from him, but strain and hunger made him very weary; Yahan was also weary, and very cold. They slogged along, for there was nothing else to do. They forded a creek, plugged up the bank through coarse grass and blowing snow, and at the top came face to face with a man.

"Houf!" he said, staring in surprise and then in wonder. For what he saw was two men walking in a snowstorm, one blue-lipped and shivering in ragged furs, the other one stark naked. "Ha, Houf!" he said again. He was a tall, bony, bowed, bearded man with a wild look in his dark eyes. "Ha you, there!" he said in the Olgyior speech, "you'll freeze to death!"

"We had to swim—our boat sank," Yahan improvised promptly. "Have you a house with a fire in it, hunter of pelliunur?"

"You were crossing the sound from the south?"

The man looked troubled, and Yahan replied with a vague gesture, "We're from the east—we came to buy pelliunfurs, but all our tradegoods went down in the water."

"Hanh, hanh," the wild man went, still troubled, but a genial streak in him seemed to win out over his fears. "Come on; I have fire and food," he said, and, turning, he jigged off into the thin, gusting snow. Following, they came soon to his hut, perched on a slope between the forested ridge and the sound. Inside and out it was like any winter hut of the midmen of the forests and hills of Angien, and Yahan squatter down before the fire with a sigh of frank relief, as if at home. That reassured their host better than any ingenious explanations. "Build up the fire, lad," he said, and he gave Rocannon a homespun cloak to wrap himself in.

Throwing off his own cloak, he set a clay bowl of stew in the ashes to warm, and hunkered down companionably with them, rolling his eyes at one and then the other. "Always snows this time of year, and it'll snow harder soon. Plenty of room for you; there's three of us winter here. The others will be in tonight or tomorrow or soon enough;

they'll be staying out this snowfall up on the ridge where they were hunting. Pelliun hunters we are, as you saw by my whistles, eh lad?" He touched the set of heavy wooden panpipes dangling at his belt, and grinned. He had a wild, fierce, foolish look to him, but his hospitality was tangible. He gave them their fill of meat stew, and when the evening darkened, told them to get their rest. Rocannon lost no time. He rolled himself up in the stinking furs of the bed-niche, and slept like a baby.

In the morning snow still fell, and the ground now was white and featureless. Their host's companions had not come back. "They'll have spent the night over across the Spine, in Timash village. They'll come along when it clears."

"The Spine—that's the arm of the sea there?"

"No, that's the sound—no villages across it! The Spine's the ridge, the hills up above us here. Where do you come from, anyhow? You talk like us here, mostly, but your uncle don't."

Yahan glanced apologetically at Rocannon, who had been asleep while acquiring a nephew. "Oh—he's from the Backlands; they talk differently. We call that water the sound, too. I wish I knew a fellow with a boat to bring us across it."

"You want to go south?"

"Well, now that all our goods are gone, we're nothing here but beggars. We'd better try to get home."

"There's a boat down on the shore, a ways from here. We'll see about that when the weather clears. I'll tell you, lad, when you talk so cool about going south my blood gets cold. There's no man dwelling between the sound and the great mountains, that ever I heard of, unless it's the Ones not talked of. And that's all old stories, and who's to say if there's any mountains even? I've been over on the other side of the sound—there's not many men can tell you that. Been there myself, hunting, in the hills. There's plenty of pelliunur there, near the water. But no villages. No men. None. And I wouldn't stay the night."

"We'll just follow the southern shore eastward," Yahan said indifferently, but with a perplexed look; his inventions were forced into further complexity with every question.

But his instinct to lie had been correct— "At least you didn't sail from the north!" their host, Piai, rambled on, sharpening his long, leaf-bladed knife on a whetstone as he talked. "No men at all across the sound, and across the sea only mangy fellows that serve as slaves to the Yellowheads. Don't your people know about them? In the north country over the sea there's a race of men with yellow heads. It's true. They say that they live in houses high as trees, and carry silver swords, and ride between the wings of windsteeds! I'll believe that when I see it. Windsteed fur brings a good price over on the coast, but the beasts are dangerous to hunt, let alone taming one and riding it. You can't believe all people tell in tales. I make a good enough living out of pelliun furs. I can bring the beasts from a day's flight around. Listen!" He put his panpipes to his hairy lips and blew, very faintly at first, a half-heard, halting plaint that swelled and changed, throbbing and breaking between notes, rising into an almost-melody that was a wild beast's cry. The chill went up Rocannon's back; he had heard that tune in the forests of Hallan. Yahan, who had been trained as a huntsman, grinned with excitement and cried out as if on the hunt and sighting the quarry, "Sing! sing! she rises there!" He and Piai spent the rest of the afternoon swapping hunting-stories, while outside the snow still fell, windless now and steady.

The next day dawned clear. As on a morning of coldyear, the sun's ruddy-white brilliance was blinding on the snow-whitened hills. Before midday Piai's two companions arrived with a few of the downy gray pelliun-furs. Black-browed, strapping men like all those southern Olgyior, they seemed still wilder than Piai, wary as animals of the strangers, avoiding them, glancing at them only sideways.

"They call my people slaves," Yahan said to Rocannon

when the others were outside the hut for a minute. "But I'd rather be a man serving men than a beast hunting beasts, like these." Rocannon raised his hand, and Yahan was silent as one of the Southerners came in, glancing sidelong at them, unspeaking.

"Let's go," Rocannon muttered in the Olgyior tongue, which he had mastered a little more of these last two days. He wished they had not waited till Piai's companions had come, and Yahan also was uneasy. He spoke to Piai, who had just come in:

"We'll be going now—this fair weather should hold till we get around the inlet. If you hadn't sheltered us we'd never have lived through these two nights of cold. And I never would have heard the pelliun-song so played. May all your hunting be fortunate!"

But Piai stood still and said nothing. Finally he hawked, spat on the fire, rolled his eyes, and growled, "Around the inlet? Didn't you want to cross by boat? There's a boat. It's mine. Anyhow, I can use it. We'll take you over the water."

"Six days walking that'll save you," the shorter newcomer, Karmik, put in.

"It'll save you six days walking," Piai repeated. "We'll take you across in the boat. We can go now."

"All right," Yahan replied after glancing at Rocannon; there was nothing they could do.

"Then let's go," Piai grunted, and so abruptly, with no offer of provision for the way, they left the hut, Piai in the lead and his friends bringing up the rear. The wind was keen, the sun bright; though snow remained in sheltered places, the rest of the ground ran and squelched and glittered with the thaw. They followed the shore westward for a long way, and the sun was set when they reached a little cove where a rowboat lay among rocks and reeds out on the water. Red of sunset flushed the water and the western sky; above the red glow the little moon Heliki gleamed waxing, and in the darkening east the Greatstar, Fomalhaut's distant companion, shone like an opal. Under the brilliant sky, over the brilliant water, the long hilly shores ran featureless and dark.

"There's the boat," said Piai, stopping and facing them, his face red with the western light. The other two came and stood in silence beside Rocannon and Yahan.

"You'll be rowing back in darkness," Yahan said.

"Greatstar shines; it'll be a light night. Now, lad, there's the matter of paying us for our rowing you."

"Ah," said Yahan.

"Piai knows—we have nothing. This cloak is his gift," said Rocannon, who, seeing how the wind blew, did not care if his accent gave them away.

"We are poor hunters. We can't give gifts," said Karmik, who had a softer voice and a saner, meaner look than Piai and the other one.

"We have nothing," Rocannon repeated. "Nothing to pay for the rowing. Leave us here."

Yahan joined in, saying the same thing more fluently, but Karmik interrupted: "You're wearing a bag around your neck, stranger. What's in it?"

"My soul," said Rocannon promptly.

They all stared at him, even Yahan. But he was in a poor position to bluff, and the pause did not last. Karmik put his hand on his leaf-bladed hunting knife, and moved closer; Piai and the other imitated him. "You were in Zgama's fort," he said. "They told a long tale about it in Timash village. How a naked man stood in a burning fire, and burned Zgama with a white stick, and walked out of the fort wearing a great jewel on a gold chair around his neck. The said it was magic and spells. I think they are all fools. Maybe you can't be hurt. But this one—" He grabbed Yahan lightning-quick by his long hair, twisted his head back and sideways, and brought the knife up against his throat. "Boy, you tell this stranger you travel with to pay for your lodging—eh?"

They all stood still. The red dimmed on the water, the Greatstar brightened in the east, the cold wind blew past them down the shore.

"We won't hurt the lad," Piai growled, his fierce face twisted and frowning. "We'll do what I said, we'll row you over the sound—only pay us. You didn't say you had gold to pay with. You said you'd lost all your gold. You slept under my roof. Give us the thing and we'll row you across."

"I will give it—over there," Rocannon said, pointing across the sound.

"No," Karmik said.

Yahan, helpless in his hands, had not moved a muscle; Rocannon could see the beating of the artery in this throat, against which the knife-blade lay.

"Over there," he repeated grimly, and tilted his driftwood walking stick forward a little in case the sight of it might impress them. "Row us across; I give you the thing. This I tell you. But hurt him and you die here, now. This I tell you!"

"Karmik, he's a pedan," Piai muttered. "Do what he says. They were under the roof with me, two nights. Let the boy go. He promises the thing you want."

Karmik looked scowling from him to Rocannon and said at last, "Throw that white stick away. Then we'll take you across."

"First let the boy go," said Rocannon, and when Karmik released Yahan, he laughed in his face and tossed the stick high, end over end, out into the water.

Knives drawn, the three huntsmen herded him and Yahan to the boat; they had to wade out and climb in her from the slippery rocks on which dull-red ripples broke. Piai and the third man rowed, Karmik sat knife in hand behind the passengers.

"Will you give him the jewel?" Yahan whispered in the Common Tongue, which these Olgyior of the peninsula did not use.

Rocannon nodded.

Yahan's whisper was very hoarse and shaky. "You jump and swim with it, Lord. Near the south shore. They'll let me go, when it's gone—"

"They'd slit your throat. Shh."

"They're casting spells, Karmik," the third man was saying. "They're going to sink the boat—"

"Row, you rotten fish-spawn. You, be still, or I'll cut the boy's neck."

Rocannon sat patiently on the thwart, watching the water turn misty gray as the shores behind and before them receded into night. Their knives could not hurt him, but they could kill Yahan before he could do much to them. He could have swum for it easy enough, but Yahan could not swim. There was no choice. At least they were getting the ride they were paying for.

Slowly the dim hills of the southern shore rose and took on substance. Faint gray shadows dropped westward and few stars came out in the gray sky; the remote solar brilliance of the Greatstar dominated even the moon Heliki, now in its waning cycle. They could hear the sough of waves against the shore. "Quit rowing," Karmik ordered, and to Rocannon: "Give me the thing now."

"Closer to shore," Rocannon said impassively.

"I can make it from here, Lord," Yahan muttered shakily. "There are reeds sticking up ahead there—"

The boat moved a few oarstrokes ahead and halted again.

"Jump when I do," Rocannon said to Yahan, and then slowly rose and stood up on the thwart. He unsealed the neck of the suit he had worn so long now, broke the leather cord around his neck with a jerk, tossed the bag that held the sapphire and its chain into the bottom of the boat, resealed the suit and in the same instant dived.

He stood with Yahan a couple of minutes later among the rocks of the shore, watching the boat, a blackish blur in the gray quarter-light on the water, shrinking.

"Oh may they rot, may they have worms in their bowels and their bones turn to slime," Yahan said, and began to cry. He had been badly scared, but more than the reaction from fear broke down his self-control. To see a "lord" toss away a jewel worth a kingdom's ransom to save a midman's life, his life, was to see all order subverted, admitting unbearable responsibility. "It was wrong, Lord!" he cried out. "It was wrong!"

"To buy your life with a rock? Come on, Yahan, get a hold of yourself. You'll freeze if we don't get a fire going. Have you got your drill? There's a lot of brushwood up this way. Get a move on!"

They managed to get a fire going there on the shore, and built it up till it drove back the night and the still, keen cold. Rocannon had given Yahan the huntsman's fur cape, and huddling in it the young man finally went to sleep. Rocannon sat keeping the fire burning, uneasy and with no wish to sleep. His own heart was heavy that he had had to throw away the necklace, not because it was valuable, but because once he had given it to Semley, whose remembered beauty had brought him, over all the years, to this world; because Haldre had given it to him, hoping, he knew, thus to buy off the shadow, the early death she feared for her son. Maybe it was as well the thing was gone, the weight, the danger of its beauty. And maybe, if worst came to worst, Mogien would never know that it was gone; because Mogien would not find him, or was already dead. . . . He put that thought aside. Mogien was looking for him and Yahan—that must be his assumption. He would look for them going south. For what plan had they ever had, except to go south—there to find the enemy, or, if all his guesses had been wrong, not to find the enemy? But with or without Mogien, he would go south.

They set out at dawn, climbing the shoreline hills in the twilight, reaching the top of them as the rising sun revealed a high, empty plain running sheer to the horizon, streaked with the long shadows of bushes. Piai had been right, apparently, when he'd said nobody lived south of the sound. At least Mogien would be able to see them from miles off. They started south.

It was cold, but mostly clear. Yahan wore what clothes they had, Rocannon his suit. They crossed creeks angling down toward the sound now and then, often enough to keep them from thirst. That day and next day they went on, living on the roots of a plant called peya and on a couple of stump-winged, hop-flying, coney-like creatures that Yahan knocked out of the air with a stick and cooked on a fire of twigs lit with his firedrill. They saw no other living thing. Clear to the sky the high grasslands stretched, level, treeless, roadless, silent.

Oppressed by immensity, the two men sat by their tiny fire in the vast dusk, saying nothing. Overhead at long intervals, like the beat of a pulse in the night, came a soft cry very high in the air. They were barilor, great wild cousins of the tamed herilor, making their northward spring migration. The stars for a hand's breadth would be blotted out by the great flocks, but never more than a single voice called, brief, a pulse on the wind.

"Which of the stars do you come from, Olhor?" Yahan asked softly, gazing up.

"I was born on a world called Hain by my mother's people, and Davenant by my father's. You call its sun the Winter Crown. But I left it long ago. . . ."

"You're not all one people, then, the Starfolk?"

"Many hundred peoples. By blood I'm entirely of my mother's race; my father, who was a Terran, adopted me. This is the custom when people of different species, who cannot conceive children, marry. As if one of your kin should marry a Fian woman."

"This does not happen," Yahan said stiffly.

"I know. But Terran and Davenanter are as alike as you and I. Few worlds have so many different races as this one. Most often there is one, much like us, and the rest are beasts without speech."

"You've seen many worlds," the young man said dreamily, trying to conceive of it.

"Too many," said the older man. "I'm forty, by your years; but I was born a hundred and forty years ago. A hundred years I've lost without living them, between the worlds. If I went back to Davenant or Earth, the men and women I knew would be a hundred years dead. I can only go on; or stop, somewhere—What's that?" The sense of some presence seemed to silence even the hissing of wind through grass. Something moved at the edge of the fire-light—a great shadow, a darkness. Rocannon knelt tensely; Yahan sprang away from the fire.

Nothing moved. Wind hissed in the grass in the gray starlight. Clear around the horizon the stars shone, unbroken by any shadow.

The two rejoined at the fire. "What was it?" Rocannon asked.

Yahan shook his head. "Piai talked of . . . something . . ."

They slept patchily, trying to spell each other keeping watch. When the slow dawn came they were very tired. They sought tracks or marks where the shadow had seemed to stand, but the young grass showed nothing. They stamped out their fire and went on, heading southward by the sun.

They had thought to cross a stream soon, but they did not. Either the stream-courses now were running north-south, or there simply were no more. The plain or pampa that seemed never to change as they walked had been becoming always a little dryer, a little grayer. This morning they saw none of the peya bushes, only the coarse gray-green grass going on and on.

At noon Rocannon stopped.

"It's no good, Yahan," he said.

Yahan rubbed his neck, looking around, then turned his gaunt, tired young face to Rocannon. "If you want to go on, Lord, I will."

"We can't make it without water or food. We'll steal a boat on the coast and go back to Hallan. This is no good. Come on.

Rocannon turned and walked northward. Yahan came along beside him. The high spring sky burned blue, the wind hissed endlessly in the endless grass. Rocannon went along steadily, his shoulders a little bent, going step by step into permanent exile and defeat. He did not turn when Yahan stopped.

"Windsteeds!"

Then he looked up and saw them, three great gryphon-cats circling down upon them, claws outstretched, wings black against the hot blue sky.

PART TWO: The Wanderer

VI

MOGIEN LEAPED OFF his steed before it had its feet on the ground, ran to Rocannon and hugged him like a brother. His voice rang with delight and relief. "By Hendin's lance, Starlord! why are you marching stark naked across this desert? How did you get so far south by walking north? Are you—" Mogien met Yahan's gaze, and stopped short.

Rocannon said, "Yahan is my bondsman."

Mogien said nothing. After a certain struggle with himself he began to grin, then he laughed out loud. "Did you learn our customs in order to steal my servants, Rokanan? But who stole your clothes?"

"Olhor wears more skins than one," said Kyo, coming with his light step over the grass. "Hail, Firelord! Last night I heard you in my mind."

"Kyo led us to you," Mogien confirmed. "Since we set foot on Fiern's shore ten days ago he never spoke a word, but last night, on the bank of the sound, when Lioka rose, he listened to the moonlight and said, 'There! Come daylight we flew where he had pointed, and so found you."

"Where is Iot?" Rocannon asked, seeing only Raho stand holding the windsteeds' reins. Mogien with unchanging face replied, "Dead. The Olgyior came on us in the fog on the beach. They had only stones for weapons, but they were many. Iot was killed, and you were lost. We hid in a cave in the seacliffs till the steeds would fly again. Raho went forth and heard tales of a stranger who stood in a burning fire unburnt, and wore a blue jewel. So when the steeds would fly we went to Zgama's fort, and not finding you we dropped fire on his wretched roofs and drove his herds into the forests, and then began to look for you along the banks of the sound."

"The jewel, Mogien," Rocannon interrupted; "the Eye of Sea—I had to buy our lives with it. I gave it away."

"The jewel?" said Mogien, staring. "Semley's jewel—you gave it away? Not to buy your life—who can harm you? To buy that worthless life, that disobedient halfman? You hold my heritage cheap! Here, take the thing; it's not so easily lost!" He spun something up in the air with a laugh, caught it, and tossed it glittering to Rocannon, who stood and gaped at it, the blue stone burning in his hand, the golden chain.

"Yesterday we met two Olgyior, and one dead one, on the other shore of the sound, and we stopped to ask about a naked traveler they might have seen going by with his worthless servant. One of them groveled on his face and told us the story, and so I took the jewel from the other one. And his life along with it, because he fought. Then we knew you had crossed the sound; and Kyo brought us straight to you. But why were you going northward, Rokanan?"

"To—to find water."

"There's a stream to the west," Raho put in. "I saw it just before we saw you."

"Let's go to it. Yahan and I haven't drunk since last night."

They mounted the windsteeds, Yahan with Raho, Kyo in his old place behind Rocannon. The wind-bowed grass dropped away beneath them, and they skimmed southwestward between the vast plain and the sun.

They camped by the stream that wound clear and slow among flowerless grasses. Rocannon could at last take off the impermasuit, and dressed in Mogien's spare shirt and cloak. They ate hardbread brought from Tolen, peya roots, and four of the stump-winged coneys shot by Raho and by Yahan, who was full of joy when he got his hands on a bow again. The creatures out here on the plain almost flew upon the arrows, and let the windsteeds snap them up in flight, having no fear. Even the tiny green and violet and yellow creatures called kilar, insect-like with transparent buzzing wings, though they were actually tiny marsupials, here were fearless and curious, hovering about one's head peering with round gold eyes, lighting on one's hand or knee a moment and skimming distractingly off again. It looked as if all this immense grassland were void of intelligent life. Mogien said they had seen no sign of men or other beings as they had flown above the plain.

"We thought we saw some creature last night, near the fire," Rocannon said hesitantly, for what had they seen? Kyo looked around at him from the cooking-fire; Mogien, unbuckling his belt that held the double swords, said nothing.

They broke camp at first light and all day rode the wind between plain and sun. Flying above the plain was as pleasant as walking across it had been hard. So passed the following day, and just before evening, as they looked out for one of the small streams that rarely broke the expanse of grass, Yahan turned in his saddle and called across the wind, "Olhor! See ahead!" Very far ahead, due south, a faint ruffling or crimping of gray broke the smooth horizon.

"The mountains!" Rocannon said, and as he spoke he heard Kyo behind him draw breath sharply, as if in fear.

During the next day's flight the flat pampas gradually rose into low swells and rolls of land, vast waves on a quiet sea. High-piled clouds drifted northward above them now and then, and far ahead they could see the land tilting upward, growing dark and broken. By evening the mountains were clear; when the plain was dark the remote, tiny peaks in the south still shone bright gold for a long time. From those far peaks as they faded, the moon Lioka rose and sailed up like a great, hurrying, yellow star. Feni and Feli were already shining, moving in more stately fashion from east to west. Last of the four rose Heliki and pursued the others, brightening and dimming in a half-hour cycle, brightening and dimming. Rocannon lay on his back and watched, through the high black stems of grass, the slow and radiant complexity of the lunar dance.

Next morning when he and Kyo went to mount the gray-striped windsteed Yahan cautioned him, standing at the beast's head: "Ride him with care today, Olhor." The windsteed agreed with a cough and a long snarl, echoed by Mogien's gray.

"What ails them?"

"Hunger!" said Raho, reining in his white steed hard. "They got their fill of Zgama's herilor, but since we started across this plain there's been no big game, and these hop-flyers are only a mouthful to 'em. Belt in your cloak, Lord Olhor—if it blows within reach of your steed's jaws you'll be his dinner." Raho, whose brown hair and skin testified to the attraction one of his grandmothers had exerted on some Angyar nobleman, was more brusque and mocking than most midmen. Mogien never rebuked him, and Raho's harshness did not hide his passionate loyalty to his lord. A man near middle age, he plainly thought this journey a fool's errand, and as plainly had never thought to do anything but go with his young lord into any peril.

Yahan handed up the reins and dodged back from Rocannon's steed, which leaped like a released spring into the air. All that day the three steeds flew wildly, tirelessly, toward the hunting-grounds they sensed or scented to the south, and a north wind hastened them on. Forested foothills rose always darker and clearer under the floating barrier of mountains. Now there were trees on the plain, clumps and groves like islands in the swelling sea of grass. The groves thickened into forests broken by green parkland. Before dusk they came down by a little sedgy lake among wooded hills. Working fast and gingerly, the two midmen stripped all packs and harness off the steeds, stood back and let them go. Up they shot, bellowing, wide wings beating, flew off in three different directions over the hills, and were gone.

"They'll come back when they've fed," Yahan told Rocannon, "or when Lord Mogien blows his still whistle."

"Sometimes they bring mates back with them—wild ones," Raho added, baiting the tenderfoot.

Mogien and the midmen scattered, hunting hop-flyers or whatever else turned up; Rocannon pulled some fat peya-roots and put them to roast wrapped in their leaves in the ashes of the campfire. He was expert at making do with what any land offered, and enjoyed it; and these days of great flights between dusk and dusk, of constant barely-assuaged hunger, of sleep on the bare ground in the wind of spring, had left him very fine-drawn, tuned and open to every sensation and impression. Rising, he saw that Kyo had wandered down to the lake-edge and was standing there, a slight figure no taller than the reeds that grew far out into the water. He was looking up at the mountains that towered gray across the south, gathering around their high heads all the clouds and silence of the sky. Rocannon, coming up beside him, saw in his face a look both desolate and eager. He said without turning, in his light hesitant voice, "Olhor, you have again the jewel."

"I keep trying to give it away," Rocannon said, grinning.

"Up there," the Fian said, "you must give more than gold and stones. . . . What will you give, Olhor, there in the cold, in the high place, the gray place? From the fire to the cold. . . ." Rocannon heard him, and watched him, yet did not see his lips move. A chill went through him and he closed his mind, retreating from the touch of a strange sense into his own humanity, his own identity. After a minute Kyo turned, calm and smiling as usual, and spoke in his usual voice. "There are Fiia beyond these foothills, beyond the forests, in green valleys. My people like the valleys, even here, the sunlight and the low places. We may find their villages in a few days' flight."

This was good news to the others when Rocannon reported it. "I thought we were going to find no speaking beings here. A fine, rich land to be so empty," Raho said.

Watching a pair of the dragonfly-like kilar dancing like

winged amethysts above the lake, Mogien said. "It was not always empty. My people crossed it long ago, in the years before the heroes, before Hallan was built or high Oynhall, before Hendin struck the great stroke or Kirfiel died on Orren Hill. We came in boats with dragonheads from the south, and found in Angien a wild folk hiding in woods and sea-caves, a white-faced folk. You know the song, Yahan, the Lay of Orhogien—

> Riding the wind,
> walking the grass,
> skimming the sea,
> toward the star Brehen
> on Lioka's path . . .

Lioka's path is from the south to the north. And the battles in the song tell how we Angyar fought and conquered the wild hunters, the Olgyior, the only ones of our race in Angien; for we're all one race, the Liuar. But the song tells nothing of those mountains. It's an old song; perhaps the beginning is lost. Or perhaps my people came from these foothills. This is a fair country—woods for hunting and hills for herds and heights for fortresses. Yet no men seem to live here now. . . ."

Yahan did not play his silver-strung lyre that night; and they all slept uneasily, maybe because the windsteeds were gone, and the hills were so deathly still, as if no creature dared move at all by night.

Agreeing that their camp by the lake was too boggy, they moved on next day, taking it easy and stopping often to hunt and gather fresh herbs. At dusk they came to a hill the top of which was humped and dented, as if under the grass lay the foundations of a fallen building. Nothing was left, yet they could trace or guess where the flightcourt of a little fortress had been, in years so long gone no legend told of it. They camped there, where the windsteeds would find them readily when they returned.

Late in the long night Rocannon woke and sat up. No

moon but little Lioka shone, and the fire was out. They had set no watch. Mogien was standing about fifteen feet away, motionless, a tall vague form in the starlight. Rocannon sleepily watched him, wondering why his cloak made him look so tall and narrow-shouldered. That was not right. The Angyar cloak flared out at the shoulders like a pagoda-roof, and even without his cloak Mogien was notably broad across the chest. Why was he standing there so stall and stooped and lean?

The face turned slowly, and it was not Mogien's face.

"Who's that?" Rocannon asked, starting up, his voice thick in the dead silence. Beside him Raho sat up, looked around, grabbed his bow and scrambled to his feet. Behind the tall figure something moved slightly—another like it. All around them, all over the grass-grown ruins in the starlight, stood tall, lean, silent forms, heavily cloaked, with bowed heads. By the cold fire only he and Raho stood.

"Lord Mogien!" Raho shouted.

No answer.

"Where is Mogien? What people are you? Speak—"

They made no answer, but they began slowly to move forward. Raho nocked an arrow. Still they said nothing, but all at once they expanded weirdly, their cloaks sweeping out on both sides, and attacked from all directions at once, coming in slow, high leaps, As Rocannon fought them he fought to waken from the dream—it must be a dream; their slowness, their silence, it was all unreal, and he could not feel them strike him. But he was wearing his suit. He heard Raho cry out desperately, "Mogien!" The attackers had forced Rocannon down by sheer weight and numbers, and then before he could struggle free again he was lifted up head downward, with a sweeping, sickening movement. As he writhed, trying to get loose from the many hands holding him, he saw starlit hills and woods swinging and rocking beneath him—far beneath. His head swam and he gripped with both hands onto the thin limbs of the creatures that had lifted him. They were all about him, their hands holding him, the air full of black wings beating.

It went on and on, and still sometimes he struggled to wake up from this monotony of fear, the soft hissing voices about him, the multiple laboring wing-beats jolting him endlessly on. Then all at once the flight changed to a long slanting glide. The brightening east slid horribly by him, the ground tilted up at him, the many soft, strong hands holding him let go, and he fell. Unhurt, but too sick and dizzy to sit up, he lay sprawling and stared about him.

Under him was a pavement of level, polished tile. To left and right above him rose wall, silvery in the early light, high and straight and clean as if cut of steel. Behind him rose the huge dome of a building, and ahead, through a topless gateway, he saw a street of windowless silvery houses, perfectly aligned, all alike, a pure geometric perspective in the unshadowed clarity of dawn. It was a city, not a stone-age village or a bronze-age fortress but a great city, severe and grandiose, powerful and exact, the product of a high technology. Rocannon sat up, his head still swimming.

As the light grew he made out certain shapes in the dimness of the court, bundles of something; the end of one gleamed yellow. With a shock that broke his trance he saw the dark face under the shock of yellow hair. Mogien's eyes were open, staring at the sky, and did not blink.

All four of his companions lay the same, rigid, eyes open. Raho's face was hideously convulsed. Even Kyo, who had seemed invulnerable in his very fragility, lay still with his great eyes reflecting the pale sky.

Yet they breathed, in long, quiet breaths seconds apart; he put his ear to Mogien's chest and heard the heartbeat very faint and slow, as if from far away.

A sibilance in the air behind him made him cower down instinctively and hold as still as the paralyzed bodies around him. Hands tugged at his shoulders and legs. He was turned over, and lay looking up into a face; a large, long face, somber and beautiful. The dark head was hairless, lacking even eyebrows. Eyes of clear gold looked out between wide, lashless lids. The mouth, small and delicately carved, was closed. The soft, strong hands were at his jaw, forcing his own mouth open. Another tall form bent over him, and he coughed and choked as something was poured down his throat—warm water, sickly and stale. The two great beings let him go. He got to his feet, spitting, and said, "I'm all right, let me be!" But their backs were already turned. They were stooping over Yahan, one forcing open his jaws, the other pouring in a mouthful of water from a long, silvery vase.

They were very tall, very thin, semi-humanoid; hard and delicate, moving rather awkwardly and slowly on the ground, which was not their element. Narrow chests projected between the shoulder-muscles of long, soft wings that fell curving down their backs like gray capes. The legs were thin and short, and the dark, noble heads seemed stooped forward by the upward jut of the wingblades.

Rocannon's *Handbook* lay under the fog-bound waters of the channel, but his memory shouted at him: *High Intelligence Life Forms, Unconfirmed Species* ?4: *Large humanoids said to inhabit extensive towns* (?). And he had the luck to confirm it, to get the first sight of a new species, a new high culture, a new member for the League. The clean, precise beauty of the buildings, the impersonal charity of the two great angelic figures who brought water, their kingly silence, it all awed him. He had never seen a race like this on any world. He came to the pair, who were giving Kyo water, and asked with diffident courtesy, "Do you speak the Common Tongue, winged lords?"

They did not heed him. They went quietly with their soft, slightly crippled ground-gait to Raho and forced water into his contorted mouth. It ran out again and down his cheeks. They moved on to Mogien, and Rocannon followed them. "Hear me!" he said, getting in front of them, but stopped: it came on him sickeningly that the wide golden eyes were blind, that they were blind and deaf. For they did not answer or glance at him, but walked away, tall, aerial, the soft wings cloaking them from neck to heel. And the door fell softly to behind them.

Pulling himself together, Rocannon went to each of his companions, hoping an antidote to the paralysis might be working. There was no change. In each he confirmed the slow breath and faint heartbeat—in each except one. Raho's chest was still and his pitifully contorted face was cold. The water they had given him was still wet on his cheeks.

Anger broke through Rocannon's awed wonder. Why did the angel-men treat him and his friends like captured wild animals? He left his companions and strode across the court yard, out the topless gate into the street of the incredible city.

Nothing moved. All doors were shut. Tall and windowless, one after another, the silvery facades stood silent in the first light of the sun.

Rocannon counted six crossings before he came to the street's end: a wall. Five meters high it ran in both directions without a break; he did not follow the circumferential street to seek a gate, guessing there was none. What need had winged beings for city gates? He returned up the radial street to the central building from which he had come, the only building in the city different from and higher than the high silvery houses in their geometric rows. He reëntered the courtyard. The houses were all shut, the streets clean and empty, the sky empty, and there was no noise but that of his steps.

He hammered on the door at the inner end of the court. No response. He pushed, and it swung open.

Within was a warm darkness, a soft hissing and stirring, a sense of height and vastness. A tall form lurched past him, stopped and stood still. In the shaft of low early sunlight he had let in the door, Rocannon saw the winged being's yellow eyes close and reopen slowly. It was the sunlight that blinded them. They must fly abroad, and walk their silver streets, only in the dark.

Facing that unfathomable gaze, Rocannon took the attitude that hilfers called "GCO" for Generalised Communications Opener, a dramatic, receptive pose, and asked in Galactic, "Who is your leader?" Spoken impressively, the question usually got some response. None this time. The Winged One gazed straight at Rocannon, blinked once with an impassivity beyond disdain, shut his eyes, and stood there to all appearances sound asleep.

Rocannon's eyes had eased to the near-darkness, and he now saw, stretching off into the warm gloom under the vaults, rows and clumps and knots of the winged figures, hundreds of them, all unmoving, eyes shut.

He walked among them and they did not move.

Long ago, on Davenant, the planet of his birth, he had walked through a museum full of statues, a child looking up into the unmoving faces of the ancient Hainish gods. Summoning his courage, he went up to one and touched him—her? they could as well be females—on the arm. The golden eyes opened, and the beautiful face turned to him, dark above him in the gloom. "Hassa!" said the Winged One, and, stooping quickly, kissed his shoulder, then took three steps away, refolded its cape of wings and stood still, eyes shut.

Rocannon gave them up and went on, groping his way through the peaceful, honeyed dusk of the huge room till he found a farther doorway, open from floor to lofty ceiling. The area beyond it was a little brighter, tiny roof holes allowing a dust of golden light to sift down. The walls curved away on either hand, rising to a narrow arched vault. It seemed to be a circular passage-room surrounding the central dome, the heart of the radial city. The inner wall was wonderfully decorated with a patter of intricately linked triangles and hexagons repeated clear up to the vault. Rocannon's puzzled ethnological enthusiasm revived. These people were master builders. Every surface in the vast building was smooth and every joint precise; the conception was splendid and the execution faultless. Only a high culture could have achieved this. But never had he met a highly-cultured race so unresponsive. After all, why had they brought him and the others here? Had they, in their silent angelic arrogance, saved the wanderers from some danger of the night? Or did they use other species as slaves? If so, it was queer how they had ignored his apparent immunity to their paralyzing agent. Perhaps they communicated entirely without words; but he inclined to believe, in this unbelievable palace, that the explanations might lie in the fact of an intelligence that was simply outside human scope. He went on, finding in the inner wall of the torus-passage a third door, this time very low, so that he had to stoop, and a Winged One must have to crawl.

Inside was the same warm, yellowish, sweet-smelling gloom, but here stirring, muttering, susurrating with a steady soft murmur of voices and slight motions of innumerable bodies and dragging wings. The eye of the dome, far up, was golden. A long ramp spiraled at a gentle slant around the wall clear up to the drum of the dome. Here and there on the ramp movement was visible, and twice a figure, tiny from below, spread its wings and flew soundlessly across the great cylinder of dusty golden air. As he started across the hall to the foot of the ramp, something fell from midway up the spiral, landing with a hard dry crack. He passed close by it. It was the corpse of one of the Winged Ones. Though the impact had smashed the skull, no blood was to be seen. The body was small, the wings apparently not fully formed.

He went doggedly on and started up the ramp.

Ten meters or so above the floor he came to a triangular niche in the wall in which Winged Ones crouched, again short and small ones, with wrinkled wings. There were nine of them, grouped regularly, three and three and three at even intervals, around a large pale bulk that Rocannon peered at a while before he made out the muzzle and the open, empty eyes. It was a windsteed, alive, paralyzed. The little delicately carved mouths of nine Winged Ones bent to it again and again, kissing it, kissing it.

Another crash on the floor across the hall. This Rocannon glanced at as he passed at a quiet run. It was the drained withered body of a barilo.

He crossed the high ornate torus-passage and threaded his way as quickly and softly as he could among the sleep-standing figures in the hall. He came out into the courtyard. It was empty. Slanting white sunlight shone on the pavement. His companions were gone. They had been dragged away from the larvae, there in the domed hall, to suck dry.

VII

ROCANNON'S KNEES gave way. He sat down on the polished red pavement, and tried to repress his sick fear enough to think what to do. What to do. He must go back into the dome and try to bring out Mogien and Yahan and Kyo. At the thought of going back in there among the tall angelic figures whose noble heads held brains degenerated or specialized to the level of insects, he felt a cold prickling at the back of his neck; but he had to do it. His friends were in there and he had to get them out. Were the larvae and their nurses in the dome sleepy enough to let him? He quit asking himself questions. But first he must check the outer wall all the way around, for if there was no gate, there was no use. He could not carry his friends over a fifteen-foot wall.

There were probably three castes, he thought as he went down the silent perfect street: nurses for the larvae in the dome, builders and hunters in the outer rooms, and in these houses perhaps the fertile ones, the egglayers and hatchers. The two that had given water would be nurses, keeping the paralyzed prey alive till the larvae sucked it dry. They had given water to dead Raho. How could he not have seen that they were mindless? He had wanted to think them intelligent because they looked so angelically human. *Strike Species* ?4, he told his drowned *Handbook,* savagely. Just then, something dashed across the street at the next crossing—a low, brown creature, whether large or small he could not tell in the unreal perspective of identical housefronts. It clearly was no part of the city. At least the angel-insects had vermin infesting their fine hive. He went on quickly and steadily through the utter silence, reached the outer wall, and turned left along it.

A little way ahead of him, close to the jointless silvery base of the wall, crouched one of the brown animals. On all fours it came no higher than his knee. Unlike most low-intelligence animals on this planet, it was wingless. It crouched there looking terrified, and he simply detoured around it, trying not to frighten it into defiance, and went on. As far as he could see ahead there was no gate in the curving wall.

"Lord," cried a faint voice from nowhere. "Lord!"

"Kyo!" he shouted, turning, his voice clapping off the walls. Nothing moved. White walls, black shadows, straight lines, silence.

The little brown animal came hopping toward him. "Lord," it cried thinly, "Lord, O come, come. O come, Lord!"

Rocannon stood staring. The little creature sat down on its strong haunches in front of him. It panted, and its heartbeat shook its furry chest, against which tiny black hands were folded. Black, terrified eyes looked up at him. It repeated in quavering Common Speech, "Lord . . ."

Roçannon knelt. His thoughts raced as he regarded the creature; at last he said very gently, "I do not know what to call you."

"O come," said the little creature, quavering. "Lords—lords. Come!"

"The other lords—my friends?"

"Friends," said the brown creature. "Friends. Castle. Lords, castle, fire, windsteed, day, night, fire. O come!"

"I'll come," said Rocannon.

It hopped off at once, and he followed. Back down the radial street it went, then one side-street to the north, and in one of the twelve gates of the dome. There in the red-paved court lay his four companions as he had left them. Later on, when he had time to think, he realized that he had come out from the dome into a different courtyard and so missed them.

Five more of the brown creatures waited there, in a

rather ceremonious group near Yahan. Rocannon knelt again to minimize his height and made as good a bow as he could. "Hail, small lords," he said.

"Hail, hail," said all the furry little people. Then one, whose fur was black around the muzzle, said, "Kiemhrir."

"You are the Kiemhrir?" They bowed in quick imitation of his bow. "I am Rokanan Olhor. We come from the north, from Angien, from Hallan Castle."

"Castle," said Blackface. His tiny piping voice trembled with earnestness. He pondered, scratched his head. "Days, night, years, years," he said. "Lords go. Years, years, years. . . Kiemhrir ungo." He looked hopefully at Rocannon.

"The Kiemhrir . . . stayed here?" Rocannon asked.

"Stay!" cried Blackface with surprising volume. "Stay! Stay!" And the others all murmured as if in delight, "Stay. . ."

"Day," Blackface said decisively, pointing up at this day's sun, "lords come. Go?"

"Yes. we would go. Can you help us?"

"Help!" said the Kiemher, latching onto the word in the same delighted, avid way. "Help go. Lord, stay!"

So Rocannon stayed: sat and watched the Kiemhrir go to work. Blackface whistled, and soon about a dozen more came cautiously hopping in. Rocannon wondered where in the mathematical neatness of the hive-city they found places to hide and live; but plainly they did, and had storerooms too, for one came carrying in its little black hands a white spheroid that looked very like an egg. It was an eggshell used as a vial; Blackface took it and carefully loosened its top. In it was a thick, clear fluid. He spread a little of this on the puncture-wounds in the shoulders of the unconscious men; then, while others tenderly and fearfully lifted the men's heads, he poured a little of the fluid in their mouths. Raho he did not touch. The Kiemhrir did not speak among themselves, using only whistles and gestures, very quiet and with a touching air of courtesy.

Blackface came over to Rocannon and said reassuringly, "Lord, stay."

"Wait? Surely."

"Lord," said the Kiemher with a gesture towards Raho's body, and then stopped.

"Dead," Rocannon said.

"Dead, dead," said the little creature. He touched the base of his neck, and Rocannon nodded.

The silver-walled court brimmed with hot light. Yahan, lying near Rocannon, drew a long breath.

The Kiemhrir sat on their haunches in a half-circle behind their leader. To him Rocannon said, "Small lord, may I know your name?"

"Name," the black-faced one whispered. The others all were very still. "Liuar," he said, the old word Mogien had used to mean both nobles and midmen, or what the *Handbook* called Species II. "Liuar, Fiia, Gdemiar: names. Kiemhrir: unname."

Rocannon nodded, wondering what might be implied here. The word "kiemher; kiemhrir" was in fact, he realized, only an adjective, meaning lithe or swift.

Behind him Kyo caught his breath, stirred, sat up. Rocannon went to him. The little nameless people watched with their black eyes, attentive and quiet. Yahan roused, then finally Mogien, who must have got a heavy dose of the paralytic agent, for he could not even lift his hand at first. One of the Kiemhrir shyly showed Rocannon that he could do good by rubbing Mogien's arms and legs, which he did, meanwhile explaining what had happened and where they were.

"The tapestry," Mogien whispered.

"What's that?" Rocannon asked him gently, thinking he was still confused, and the young man whispered.

"The tapestry, at home—the winged giants."

Then Rocannon remembered how he had stood with Haldre beneath a woven picture of fair-haired warriors fighting winged figures, in the Long Hall of Hallan.

Kyo, who had been watching the Kiemhrir, held out his hand. Blackface hopped up to him and put his tiny, black, thumbless hand on Kyo's long, slender palm.

"Wordmasters," said the Fian softly. "Wordlovers, the eaters of words, the nameless ones, the lithe ones, long remembering. Still you remember the words of the Tall People, O Kiemhrir?"

"Still," said Blackface.

With Rocannon's help Mogien got to his feet, looking gaunt and stern. He stood a while beside Raho, whose face was terrible in the strong white sunlight. Then he greeted the Kiemhrir, and said, answering Rocannon, that he was all right again.

"If there are no gates, we can cut footholds and climb," Rocannon said.

"Whistle for the steeds, Lord," mumbled Yahan.

The question whether the whistle might wake the creatures in the dome was too complex to put across to the Kiemhrir. Since the Winged Ones seemed entirely nocturnal, they opted to take the chance. Mogien drew a little pipe on a chain from under his cloak, and blew a blast on it that Rocannon could not hear, but that made the Kiemhrir flinch. Within twenty minutes a great shadow shot over the dome, wheeled, darted off north, and before long returned with a companion. Both dropped with a mighty fanning of wings into the courtyard: the striped windsteed and Mogien's gray. The white one they never saw again. It might have been the one Rocannon had seen on the ramp in the musty, golden dusk of the dome, food for the larvae of the angels.

The Kiemhrir were afraid of the steeds. Blackface's gentle miniature courtesy was almost lost in barely controlled panic when Rocannon tried to thank him and bid him farewell. "O fly, Lord!" he said piteously, edging away from the great, taloned feet of the windsteeds; so they lost no time in going.

An hour's windride from the hive-city their packs and the spare cloaks and furs they used for bedding, lay untouched beside the ashes of last night's fire. Partway down the hill lay three Winged Ones dead, and near them both Mogien's swords, one of them snapped off near the hilt. Mogien had waked to see the Winged Ones stooping over Yahan and Kyo. One of them had bitten him, "and I could not speak," he said. But he had fought and killed three before the paralysis brought him down. "I heard Raho call. He called to me three times, and I could not help him." He sat among the grassgrown ruins that had outlived all names and legends, his broken sword on his knees, and said nothing else.

They built up a pyre of branches and brushwood, and on it laid Raho, whom they had borne from the city, and beside him his hunting-bow and arrows. Yahan made a new fire, and Mogien set the wood alight. They mounted the windsteeds, Kyo behind Mogien and Yahan behind Rocannon, and rose spiraling around the smoke and heat of the fire that blazed in the sunlight of noon on a hilltop in the strange land.

For a long time they could see the thin pillar of smoke behind them as they flew.

The Kiemhrir had made it clear that they must move on, and keep under cover at night, or the Winged Ones would be after them again in the dark. So toward evening they came down to a stream in a deep, wooded gorge, making camp within earshot of a waterfall. It was damp, but the air was fragrant and musical, relaxing their spirits. They found a delicacy for dinner, a certain shelly, slow-moving water animal very good to eat; but Rocannon could not eat them. There was vestigial fur between the joints and on the tail; they were ovipoid mammals, like many animals here, like the Kiemhrir probably. "You eat them, Yahan. I can't shell something that might speak to me," he said, wrathful with hunger, and came to sit beside Kyo.

Kyo smiled, rubbing his sore shoulder. "If all things could be heard speaking . . ."

"I for one would starve."

"Well, the green creatures are silent," said the Fian,

patting a rough-trunked tree that leaned across the stream. Here in the south the trees, all conifers, were coming into bloom, and the forests were dusty and sweet with drifting pollen. All flowers here gave their pollen to the wind, grasses and conifers: there were no insects, no petaled flowers. Spring on the unnamed world was all in green, dark green and pale green, with great drifts of golden pollen.

Mogien and Yahan went to sleep as it grew dark, stretched out by the warm ashes; they kept no fire lest it draw the Winged Ones. As Rocannon had guessed, Kyo was tougher than the men when it came to poisons; he sat and talked with Rocannon, down on the streambank in the dark.

"You greeted the Kiemhrir as if you knew of them," Rocannon observed, and the Fian answered:

"What one of us in my village remembered, all remembered, Olhor. So many tales and whispers and lies and truths are known to us, and who knows how old some are. . . ."

"Yet you knew nothing of the Winged Ones?"

It looked as if Kyo would pass this one, but at last he said, "The Fiia have no memory for fear, Olhor. How should we? We chose. Night and caves and swords of metal we left to the Clayfolk, when our way parted from theirs, and we chose the green valleys, the sunlight, the bowl of wood. And therefore we are the Half-People. And we have forgotten, we have forgotten much!" His light voice was more decisive, more urgent this night than ever before, sounding clear through the noise of the stream below them and the noise of the falls at the head of the gorge. "Each day as we travel southward I ride into the tales that my people learn as little children, in the valleys of Angien. And all the tales I find true. But half of them all we have forgotten. The little Name-Eaters, the Kiemhrir, these are in old songs we sing from mind to mind; but not the Winged Ones. The friends, but not the enemies. The sunlight, not the dark. And I am the companion of Olhor who goes southward into the legends, bearing no sword. I ride with Olhor, who seeks to hear his enemy's voice, who has traveled through the great dark, who has seen the World hang like a blue jewel in the darkness. I am only a half-person. I cannot go farther than the hills. I cannot go into the high places with you, Olhor!"

Rocannon put his hand very lightly on Kyo's shoulder. At once the Fian fell still. They sat hearing the sound of the stream, of the falls in the night, and watching starlight gleam gray on water that ran, under drifts and whorls of blown pollen, icy cold from the mountains to the south.

Twice during the next day's flight they saw far to the east the domes and spoked streets of hive-cities. That night they kept double watch. By the next night they were high up in the hills, and a lashing cold rain beat at them all night long and all the next day as they flew. When the rain-clouds parted a little there were mountains looming over the hills now on both sides. One more rain-sodden, watch-broken night went by on the hilltops under the ruin of an ancient tower, and then in early afternoon of the next day they came down the far side of the pass into sunlight and a broad valley leading off southward into misty, mountain-fringed distances.

To their right now while they flew down the valley as if it were a great green roadway, the white peaks stood serried, remote and huge. The wind was keen and golden, and the windsteeds raced down it like blown leaves in the sunlight. Over the soft green concave below them, on which darker clumps of shrubs and trees seemed enameled, drifted a narrow veil of gray. Mogien's mount came circling back, Kyo pointing down, and they rode down the golden wind to the village that lay between hill and stream, sunlit, its small chimneys smoking. A herd of herilor grazed the slopes above it. In the center of the scattered circle of little houses, all stilts and screens and sunny porches, towered five great trees. By these the travelers landed, and the Fiia came to meet them, shy and laughing.

These villagers spoke little of the Common Tongue,

and were unused to speaking aloud at all. Yet it was like a homecoming to enter their airy houses, to eat from bowls of polished wood, to take refuge from wilderness and weather for one evening in their blithe hospitality. A strange little people, tangential, gracious, elusive: the Half-People, Kyo had called his own kind. Yet Kyo himself was no longer quite one of them. Though in the fresh clothing they gave him he looked like them, moved and gestured like them, in the group of them he stood out absolutely. Was it because as a stranger he could not freely mindspeak with them, or was it because he had, in this friendship with Rocannon, changed, having become another sort of being, more solitary, more sorrowful, more complete?

They could describe the lay of this land. Across the great range west of their valley was desert, they said; to continue south the travelers should follow the valley, keeping east of the mountains, a long way, until the range itself turned east. "Can we find passes across?" Mogien asked, and the little people smiled and said, "Surely, surely."

"And beyond the passes do you know what lies?"

"The passes are very high, very cold," said the Fiia, politely.

The travelers stayed two nights in the village to rest, and left with packs filled with waybread and dried meat given by the Fiia, who delighted in giving. After two days' flight they came to another village of the little folk, where they were again received with such friendliness that it might have been not a strangers' arrival, but a long-awaited return. As the steeds landed a group of Fian men and women came to meet them, greeting Rocannon, who was first to dismount, "Hail, Olhor!" It startled him, and still puzzled him a little after he thought that the word of course meant "wanderer," which he obviously was. Still, it was Kyo the Fian who had given him the name.

Later, farther down the valley after another long, calm

day's flight, he said to Kyo, "Among your people, Kyo did you bear no name of your own?"

"They call me 'herdsman,' or 'younger brother,' or 'runner.' I was quick in our racing."

"But those are nicknames, descriptions—like Olhor or Kiemhrir. You're great namegivers, you Fiia. You greet each comer with a nickname, Starlord, Swordbearer, Sunhaired, Wordmaster—I think the Angyar learned their love of such nicknaming from you. And yet you have no names."

"Starlord, far-traveled, ashen-haired, jewel-bearer," said Kyo, smiling;—"what then is a name?"

"Ashen-haired? Have I turned gray?—I'm not sure what a name is. My name given me at birth was Gaverel Rocannon. When I've said that, I've described nothing, yet I've named myself. And when I see a new kind of tree in this land I ask you—or Yahan and Mogien, since you seldom answer—what its name it. It troubles me, until I know its name."

"Well, it is a tree; as I am a Fian; as you are a . . . what?"

"But there are distinctions, Kyo! At each village here I ask what are those western mountains called, the range that towers over their lives from birth to death, and they say, 'Those are mountains, Olhor.' "

"So they are," said Kyo.

"But there are other mountains—the lower range to the east, along this same valley! How do you know one range from another, one being from another, without names?

Clasping his knees, the Fian gazed at the sunset peaks burning high in the west. After a while Rocannon realized that he was not going to answer.

The winds grew warmer and the long days longer as warmyear advanced and they went each day farther south. As the windsteeds were double-loaded they did not push on fast, stopping often for a day or two to hunt and to let the steeds hunt; but at last they saw the mountains curving around in front of them to meet the coastal range to the east, barring their way. The green of the valley ran up the knees of huge hills, and ceased. Much higher lay patches of green and brown-green, alpine valleys; then the gray of rock and talus; and finally, halfway up the sky, the luminous storm-ridden white of the peaks.

They came, high up in the hills, to a Fian village. Wind blew chill from the peaks across frail roofs, scattering blue smoke among the long evening light and shadows. As ever they were received with cheerful grace, given water and fresh meat and herbs in bowls of wood, in the warmth of a house, while their dusty clothes were cleaned, and their windsteeds fed and petted by tiny, quicksilver children. After supper four girls of the village danced for them, without music, their movements and footfalls so light and swift that they seemed bodiless, a play of light and dark in the glow of the fire, elusive, fleeting. Rocannon glanced with a smile of pleasure at Kyo, who as usual sat beside him. The Fian returned his look gravely and spoke: "I shall stay here, Olhor."

Rocannon checked his startled reply and for a while longer watched the dancers, the changing unsubstantial patterns of firelit forms in motion. They wove a music from silence, and a strangeness in the mind. The firelight on the wooden walls bowed and flickered and changed.

"It was foretold that the Wanderer would choose companions. For a while."

He did not know if he had spoken, or Kyo, or his memory. The words were in his mind and in Kyo's. The dancers broke apart, their shadows running quickly up the walls, the loosened hair of one swinging bright for a moment. The dance that had no music was ended, the dancers that had no more name than light and shadow were still. So between him and Kyo a pattern had come to its end, leaving quietness.

VIII

Below his windsteed's heavily beating wings Rocannon saw a slope of broken rock, a slanting chaos of boulders running down behind, tilted up ahead so that the steed's left wingtip almost brushed the rocks as it labored up and forward towards the col. He wore the battle-straps over his thighs, for updrafts and gusts sometimes blew the steeds off balance, and he wore his impermasuit for warmth. Riding behind him, wrapped in all the cloaks and furs the two of them had, Yahan was still so cold that he had strapped his wrists to the saddle, unable to trust his grip. Mogien, riding well ahead on his less burdened steed, bore the cold and altitude much better than Yahan, and met their battle with the heights with a harsh joy.

Fifteen days ago they had left the last Fian village, bidding farewell to Kyo, and set out over the foothills and lower ranges for what looked like the widest pass. The Fiia could give them no directions; at any mention of crossing the mountains they had fallen silent, with a cowering look.

The first days had gone well, but as they got high up the windsteeds began to tire quickly, the thinner air not supplying them with the rich oxygen intake they burned while flying. Higher still they met the cold and the treacherous weather of high altitudes. In the last three days they had covered perhaps fifteen kilometers, most of that distance on a blind lead. The men went hungry to give the steeds an extra ration of dried meat; this morning Rocannon had let them finish what was left in the sack, for if they did not get across the pass today they would have to drop back down to woodlands where they could hunt and rest, and start all over. They seemed now on the right way toward a pass, but from the peaks to the east a terrible thin wind blew, and the sky was getting white and heavy. Still Mogien flew ahead, and Rocannon forced his mount to follow; for in this endless cruel passage of the great heights. Mogien was his leader and he followed. He had forgotten why he wanted to cross these mountains, remembering only that he had to, that he must go south. But for the courage to do it, he depended on Mogien. "I think this is your domain," he had said to the young man last evening when they had discussed their present course; and, looking out over the great, cold view of peak and abyss, rock and snow and sky, Mogien had answered with his quick lordly certainty, "This is my domain."

He was calling now, and Rocannon tried to encourage his steed, while he peered ahead through frozen lashes seeking a break in the endless slanting chaos. There it was, an angle, a jutting roofbeam of the planet: the slope of rock fell suddenly away and under them lay a waste of white, the pass. On either side wind-scoured peaks reared on up into the thickening snowclouds. Rocannon was close enough to see Mogien's untroubled face and hear his shout, the falsetto battle-yell of the victorious warrior. He kept following Mogien over the white valley under the white clouds. Snow began to dance about them, not falling, only dancing here in its habitat, its birthplace, a dry flickering dance. Half-starved and overladen, the windsteed gasped at each lift and downbeat of its great barred wings. Mogien had dropped back so they would not lose him in the snowclouds, but still kept on, and they followed.

There was a glow in the flickering mist of snowflakes, and gradually there dawned a thin, clear radiance of gold. Pale gold, the sheer fields of snow reached downward. Then abruptly the world fell away, and the windsteeds floundered in a vast gulf of air. Far beneath, very far, clear and small, lay valleys, lakes, the glittering tongue of a glacier, green patches of forest. Rocannon's mount floundered and dropped, its wings raised, dropped like a stone so that

Yahan cried out in terror and Rocannon shut his eyes and held on.

The wings beat and thundered, beat again; the falling slowed, became again a laboring glide, and halted. The steed crouched trembling in a rocky valley. Nearby Mogien's gray beast was trying to lie down while Mogien, laughing, jumped off its back and called, "We're over, we did it!" He came up to them, his dark, vivid face bright with triumph. "Now both sides of the mountains are my domain, Rokanan! . . . This will do for our camp tonight. Tomorrow the steeds can hunt, farther down where trees grow, and we'll work down on foot. Come, Yahan."

Yahan crouched in the postillion-saddle, unable to move. Mogien lifted him from the saddle and helped him lie down in the shelter of a jutting boulder; for though the late afternoon sun shone here, it gave little more warmth than did the Greatstar, a tiny crumb of crystal in the southwestern sky; and the wind still blew bitter cold. While Rocannon unharnessed the steeds, the Angyar lord tried to help his servant, doing what he could to get him warm. There was nothing to build a fire with—they were still far above timberline. Rocannon stripped off the impermasuit and made Yahan put it on, ignoring the midman's weak and scared protests, then wrapped himself up in furs. The windsteeds and the men huddled together for mutual warmth, and shared a little water and Fian waybread. Night rose up from the vague lands below. Stars leaped out, released by darkness, and the two brighter moons shone within hand's reach.

Deep in the night Rocannon roused from blank sleep. Everything was starlit, silent, deathly cold. Yahan had hold of his arm and was whispering feverishly, shaking his arm and whispering. Rocannon looked where he pointed and saw standing on the boulder above them a shadow, an interruption in the stars.

Like the shadow he and Yahan had seen on the pampas, far back to northward, it was large and strangely vague. Even as he watched it the stars began to glimmer faintly through the dark shape, and then there was no shadow, only black transparent air. To the left of where it had been Heliki shone, faint in its waning cycle.

"It was a trick of moonlight, Yahan," he whispered. "Go back to sleep, you've got a fever."

"No," said Mogien's quiet voice beside him. "It wasn't a trick, Rokanan. It was my death."

Yahan sat up, shaking with fever. "No, Lord! not yours; it couldn't be! I saw it before, on the plains when you weren't with us—so did Olhor!"

Summoning to his aid the last shreds of common sense, of scientific moderation, of the old life's rules, Rocannon tried to speak authoritatively: "Don't be absurd," he said.

Mogien paid no attention to him. "I saw it on the plains, where it was seeking me. And twice in the hills while we sought the pass. Whose death would it be if not mine? Yours, Yahan? Are you a lord, an Angya; do you wear the second sword?"

Sick and despairing, Yahan tried to plead with him, but Mogien went on, "It's not Rokanan's, for he still follows his way. A man can die anywhere, but his own death, his true death, a lord meets only in his domain. It waits for him in the place which is his, a battlefield or a hall or a road's ends. And this is my place. From these mountains my people came, and I have come back. My second sword was broken, fighting. But listen, my death: I am Halla's heir Mogien—do you know me now?"

The thin, frozen wind blew over the rocks. Stones loomed about them, stars glittering out beyond them. One of the windsteeds stirred and snarled.

"Be still," Rocannon said. "This is all foolishness. Be still and sleep. . . ."

But he could not sleep soundly after that, and whenever he roused he saw Mogien sitting by his steed's great flank, quiet and ready, watching over the night-darkened lands.

Come daylight they let the windsteeds free to hunt in the forests below, and started to work their way down on foot. They were still very high, far above timberline, and safe only so long as the weather held clear. But before they had gone an hour they saw Yahan could not make it; it was not a hard descent, but exposure and exhaustion had taken too much out of him and he could not keep walking, let alone scramble and cling as they sometimes must. Another day's rest in the protection of Rocannon's suit might give him the strength to go on; but that would mean another night up here without fire or shelter or enough food. Mogien weighed the risks without seeming to consider them at all, and suggested that Rocannon stay with Yahan on a sheltered and sunny ledge, while he sought a descent easy enough that they might carry Yahan down, or, failing that, a shelter that might keep off snow.

After he had gone, Yahan, lying in a half stupor, asked for water. Their flask was empty. Rocannon told him to lie still, and climbed up the slanting rockface to a boulder-shadowed ledge fifteen meters or so above, where he saw some packed snow glittering. The climb was rougher than he had judged, and he lay on the ledge gasping the bright, thin air, his heart going hard.

There was a noise in his ears which at first he took to be the singing of his own blood; then near his hand he saw water running. He sat up. A tiny stream, smoking as it ran, wound along the base of a drift of hard, shadowed snow. He looked for the stream's source and saw a dark gap under the overhanging cliff: a cave. A cave was their best hope of shelter, said his rational mind, but it spoke only on the very fringe of a dark non-rational rush of feeling—of panic. He sat there unmoving in the grip of the worst fear he had ever known.

All about him the unavailing sunlight shone on gray rock. The mountain peaks were hidden by the nearer cliffs, and the lands below to the south were hidden by unbroken cloud. There was nothing at all here on this bare gray ridgepole of the world but himself, and a dark opening between boulders.

After a long time he got to his feet, went forward stepping across the steaming rivulet, and spoke to the presence which he knew waited inside that shadowy gap. "I have come," he said.

The darkness moved a little, and the dweller in the cave stood at its mouth.

It was like the Clayfolk, dwarfish and pale; like the Fiia, frail and clear-eyed; like both, like neither. The hair was white. The voice was no voice, for it sounded within Rocannon's mind while all his ears heard was the faint whistle of the wind; and there were no words. Yet it asked him what he wished.

"I do not know," the man said aloud in terror, but his set will answered silently for him: *I will go south and find my enemy and destroy him.*

The wind blew whistling; the warm stream chuckled at his feet. Moving slowly and lightly, the dweller in the cave stood aside, and Rocannon, stooping down, entered the dark place.

What do you give for what I have given you?

What must I give, Ancient One?

That which you hold dearest and would least willingly give.

I have nothing of my own on this world. What thing can I give?

A thing, a life, a chance; an eye, a hope, a return: the name need not be known. But you will cry its name aloud when it is gone. Do you give it freely?

Freely, Ancient One.

Silence and the blowing of wind. Rocannon bowed his head and came out of the darkness. As he straightened up red light struck full in his eyes, a cold red sunrise over a gray-and-scarlet sea of cloud.

Yahan and Mogien slept huddled together on the lower ledge, a heap of furs and cloaks, unstirring as Rocannon climbed down to them. "Wake up," he said softly. Yahan sat up, his face pinched and childish in the hard red dawn.

"Olhor! We thought—you were gone—we thought you had fallen—"

Mogien shook his yellow-maned head to clear it of sleep, and looked up a minute at Rocannon. Then he said hoarsely and gently, "Welcome back, Starlord, companion. We waited here for you."

"I met . . . I spoke with . . ."

Mogien raised his hand. "You have come back; I rejoice in your return. Do we go south?"

"Yes."

"Good," said Mogien. In that moment it was not strange to Rocannon that Mogien, who for so long had seemed his leader, now spoke to him as a lesser to a greater lord.

Mogien blew his whistle, but though they waited long the windsteeds did not come. They finished the last of the hard, nourishing Fian bread, and set off once more on foot. The warmth of the impermasuit had done Yahan good, and Rocannon insisted he keep it on. The young midman needed food and real rest to get his strength back, but he could get on now, and they had to get on; behind that red sunrise would come heavy weather. It was not dangerous going, but slow and wearisome. Midway in the morning one of the steeds appeared: Mogien's gray, flitting up from the forests far below. They loaded it with the saddles and harness and furs—all they carried now—and it flew along above or below or beside them as it pleased, sometimes letting out a ringing yowl as if to call its striped mate, still hunting or feasting down in the forests.

About noon they came to a hard stretch: a cliff-face sticking out like a shield, over which they would have to crawl roped together. "From the air you might see a better path for us to follow, Mogien," Rocannon suggested. "I wish the other steed would come." He had a sense of urgency; he wanted to be off this bare gray mountainside and be hidden down among trees.

"The beast was tired out when we let it go; it may not have made a kill yet. This one carried less weight over the pass. I'll see how wide this cliff is. Perhaps my steed can carry all three of us for a few bowshots." He whistled and the gray steed, with the loyal obedience that still amazed Rocannon in a beast so large and so carnivorous, wheeled around in the air and came looping gracefully up to the cliffside where they waited. Mogien swung up on it and with a shout sailed off, his bright hair catching the last shaft of sunlight that broke through thickening banks of cloud.

Still the thin, cold wind blew. Yahan crouched back in an angle of rock, his eyes closed. Rocannon sat looking out into the distance at the remotest edge of which could be sensed the fading brightness of the sea. He did not scan the immense, vague landscape that came and went between drifting clouds, but gazed at one point, south and a little east, one place. He shut his eyes. He listened, and heard.

It was a strange gift he had got from the dweller in the cave, the guardian of the warm well in the unnamed mountains; a gift that went all against his grain to ask. There in the dark by the deep warm spring he had been taught a skill of the senses that his race and the men of Earth had witnessed and studied in other races, but to which they were deaf and blind, save for brief glimpses and rare exceptions. Clinging to his humanity, he had drawn back from the totality of the power that the guardian of the well possessed and offered. He had learned to listen to the minds of one race, one kind of creature, among all the voices of all the worlds one voice: that of his enemy.

With Kyo he had had some beginnings of mindspeech; but he did not want to know his companions' minds when they were ignorant of his. Understanding must be mutual, when loyalty was, and love.

But those who had killed his friends and broken the bond of peace he spied upon, he overheard. He sat on the granite spur of a trackless mountain-peak and listened to the thoughts of men in buildings among rolling hills thousands of meters below and a hundred kilometers away. A dim chatter, a buzz and babble and confusion, a remote roil and storming of sensations and emotions. He did not know how to select voice from voice, and was dizzy among a hundred different places and positions; he listened as a young infant listens, undiscriminating. Those born with eyes and ears must learn to see and hear, to pick out a face from a double eyefull of upside-down world, to select meaning from a welter of noise. The guardian of the well had the gift, which Rocannon had only heard rumor of on one other planet, of unsealing the telepathic sense; and he had taught Rocannon how to limit and direct it, but there had been no time to learn its use, its practice. Rocannon's head spun with the impingement of alien thoughts and feelings, a thousand strangers crowded in his skull. No words came through. Mindhearing was the word the Angyar, the outsiders, used for the sense. What he "heard" was not speech but intentions, desires, emotions, the physical locations and sensual-mental directions of many different men jumbling and overlapping through his own nervous system, terrible gusts of fear and jealousy, drifts of contentment, abysses of sleep, a wild racking vertigo of half-understanding, half-sensation. And all at once out of the chaos something stood absolutely clear, a contact more definite than a hand laid on his naked flesh. Someone was coming toward him: a man whose mind had sensed his own. With this certainty came lesser impressions of speed, of confinement; of curiosity and fear.

Rocannon opened his eyes, staring ahead as if he would see before him the face of that man whose being he had sensed. He was close; Rocannon was sure he was close, and coming closer. But there was nothing to see but air and lowering clouds. A few dry, small flakes of snow whirled in the wind. To his left bulked the great bosse of rock that blocked their way. Yahan had come out beside him and was watching him, with a scared look. But he could not reassure Yahan, for that presence tugged at him and he could not break the contact. "There is . . . there is a . . . an airship," he muttered thickly, like a sleeptalker. "There!"

There was nothing where he pointed; air, cloud.

"There," Rocannon whispered.

Yahan, looking again where he pointed, gave a cry. Mogien on the gray steed was riding the wind well out from the cliff; and beyond him, far out in a scud of cloud, a larger black shape had suddenly appeared, seeming to hover or to move very slowly. Mogien flashed on downwind without seeing it, his face turned to the mountain wall looking for his companions, two tiny figures on a tiny ledge in the sweep of rock and cloud.

The black shape grew larger, moving in, its vanes clacking and hammering in the silence of the heights. Rocannon saw it less clearly than he sensed the man inside it, the uncomprehending touch of mind on mind, the intense defiant fear. He whispered to Yahan, "Take cover!" but could not move himself. The helicopter nosed in unsteadily, rags of cloud catching in its whirring vanes. Even as he watched it approach, Rocannon watched from inside it, not knowing what he looked for, seeing two small figures on the mountainside, afraid, afraid—A flash of light, a hot shock of pain, pain in his own flesh, intolerable. The mind-contact was broken, blown clean away. He was himself, standing on the ledge pressing his right hand against his chest and gasping, seeing the helicopter creep still closer, its vanes whirring with a dry loud rattle, its laser-mounted nose pointing at him.

From the right, from the chasm of air and cloud, shot a gray winged beast ridden by a man who shouted in a voice like a high, triumphant laugh. One beat of the wide gray wings drove steed and rider forward straight against the hovering machine, full speed, head on. There was a tearing sound like the edge of a great scream, and then the air was empty.

The two on the cliff crouched staring. No sound came up

from below. Clouds wreathed and drifted across the abyss.

"Mogien!"

Rocannon cried the name aloud. There was no answer. There was only pain, and fear, and silence.

IX

RAIN PATTERED HARD on a raftered roof. The air of the room was dark and clear.

Near his couch stood a woman whose face he knew, a proud, gentle, dark face crowned with gold.

He wanted to tell her that Mogien was dead, but he could not say the words. He lay there sorely puzzled, for new he recalled that Haldre of Hallan was an old woman, white-haired; and the golden-haired woman he had known was long dead; and anyway he had seen her only once, on a planet eight lightyears away, a long time ago when he had been a man named Rocannon.

He tried again to speak. She hushed him, saying in the Common Tongue though with some difference in sounds, "Be still, my lord." She stayed beside him, and presently told him in her soft voice, "This is Breygna Castle. You came here with another man, in the snow, from the heights of the mountains. You were near death and still are hurt. There will be time. . . ."

There was much time, and it slipped by vaguely, peacefully in the sound of the rain.

The next day or perhaps the next, Yahan came in to him, Yahan very thin, a little lame, his face scarred with frostbite. But a less understandable change in him was his manner, subdued and submissive. After they had talked a while Rocannon asked uncomfortably, "Are you afraid of me, Yahan?"

"I will try not to be, Lord," the young man stammered.

When he was able to go down to the Revelhall of the castle, the same awe or dread was in all faces that turned to him, though they were brave and genial faces. Gold-haired, dark-skinned, a tall-people, the old stock of which the Angyar were only a tribe that long ago had wandered north by sea: these were the Liuar, the Earthlords, living since before the memory of any race here in the foothills of the mountains and the rolling plains to the south.

At first he thought that they were unnerved simply by his difference in looks, his dark hair and pale skin; but Yahan was colored like him, and they had no dread of Yahan. They treated him as a lord among lords, which was a joy and a bewilderment to the ex-serf of Hallan. But Rocannon they treated as a lord above lords, one set apart.

There was one who spoke to him as to a man. The Lady Ganye, daughter-in-law and heiress of the castle's old lord, had been a widow for some months; her bright-haired little son was with her most of the day. Though shy, the child had no fear of Rocannon, but was rather drawn to him, and liked to ask him questions about the mountains and the northern lands and the sea. Rocannon answered whatever he asked. The mother would listen, serene and gentle as the sunlight, sometimes turning smiling to Rocannon her face that he had remembered even as he had seen it for the first time.

He asked her at last what it was they thought of him in Breygna Castle, and she answered candidly, "They think you are a god."

It was the word he had noted long since in Tolen village, *pedan.*

"I'm not," he said, dour.

She laughed a little.

"Why do they think so?" he demanded. "Do the gods of the Liuar come with gray hair and crippled hands?" The laserbeam from the helicopter had caught him in the right wrist, and he had lost the use of his right hand almost entirely.

"Why not?" said Ganye with her proud, candid smile. "But the reason is that you came *down* the mountain."

He absorbed this a while. "Tell me, Lady Ganye, do you know of . . . the guardian of the well?"

At this her face was grave. "We know tales of that people only. It is very long, nine generations of the Lords of Breygna, since Iollt the Tall went up into the high places and came down changed. We knew you had met with them, with the Most Ancient."

"How do you know?"

"In your sleep in fever you spoke always of the price, of the cost, of the gift given and its price. Iollt paid too. . . . The cost was your right hand, Lord Olhor?" she asked with sudden timidity, raising her eyes to his.

"No. I would give both my hands to have saved what I lost."

He got up and went to the window of the tower-room, looking out on the spacious country between the mountains and the distant sea. Down from the high foothills where Breygna Castle stood wound a river, widening and shining among lower hills, vanishing into hazy reaches where one could half make out villages, fields, castle towers, and once again the gleam of the river among blue rainstorms and shafts of sunlight.

"This is the fairest land I ever saw," he said. He was still thinking of Mogien, who would never see it.

"It's not so fair to me as it once was."

"Why, Lady Ganye?"

"Because of the Strangers!"

"Tell me of them, Lady."

"They came here late last winter, many of them riding in great windships, armed with weapons that burn. No one can say what land they come from; there are no tales of them at all. All the land between Viarn River and the sea is theirs now. They killed or drove out all the people of eight domains. We in the hills here are prisoners; we dare not go down even to the old pasturelands with our herds. We fought the Strangers, at first. My husband Ganhing was killed by their burning weapons." Her gaze went for a second to Rocannon's seared, crippled hand; for a second she paused. "In . . . in the time of the first thaw he was killed, and still we have no revenge. We bow our heads and avoid their lands, we the Earthlords! And there is no man to make these Strangers pay for Ganhing's death."

O lovely wrath, Rocannon thought, hearing the trumpets of lost Hallan in her voice. "They will pay, Lady Ganye; they will pay a high price. Though you knew I was no god, did you take me for quite a common man?"

"No, Lord," said she. "Not quite."

The days went by, the long days of the yearlong summer. The white slopes of the peaks above Breygna turned blue, the grain-crops in Breygna fields ripened, were cut and resown, and were ripening again when one afternoon Rocannon sat down by Yahan in the courtyard where a pair of young windsteeds were being trained. "I'm off again to the south, Yahan. You stay here."

"No, Olhor! Let me come—"

Yahan stopped, remembering perhaps that foggy beach where in his longing for adventures he had disobeyed Mogien. Rocannon grinned and said, "I'll do best alone. It won't take long, one way or the other."

"But I am your vowed servant, Olhor. Please let me come."

"Vows break when names are lost. You swore your service to Rokanan, on the other side of the mountains. In this land there are no serfs, and there is no man named Rokanan. I ask you as my friend, Yahan, to say no more to me or to anyone here, but saddle the steed of Hallan for me at daybreak tomorrow."

Loyally, next morning before sunrise Yahan stood waiting for him in the flightcourt, holding the bridle of the one remaining windsteed from Hallan, the gray striped one. It had made its way a few days after them to Breygna, half frozen and starving. It was sleek and full of spirit now, snarling and lashing its striped tail.

"Do you wear the Second Skin, Olhor?" Yahan asked in a whisper, fastening the battle-straps on Rocannon's legs. "They say the Strangers shoot fire at any man who rides near their lands."

"I'm wearing it."

"But no sword? . . ."

"No. No sword. Listen, Yahan, if I don't return, look in the wallet I left in my room. There's some cloth in it, with —with markings in it, and pictures of the land; if any of my people ever come here, give them those, will you? And also the necklace is there." His face darkened and he looked away a moment. "Give that to the Lady Ganye. If I don't come back to do it myself. Goodbye, Yahan; wish me good luck."

"May your enemy die without sons," Yahan said fiercely, in tears, and let the windsteed go. It shot up into the warm, uncolored sky of summer dawn, turned with a great rowing beat of wings, and, catching the north wind, vanished above the hills. Yahan stood watching. From a window high up in Breygna Tower a soft, dark face also watched, for a long time after it was out of sight and the sun had risen.

It was a queer journey Rocannon made, to a place he had never seen and yet knew inside and out with the varying impressions of hundreds of different minds. For though there was no seeing with the mind-sense, there was tactile sensation and perception of space and spatial relationships, of time, motion, and position. From attending to such sensations over and over for hours on end in a hundred days of practice as he sat moveless in his room in Breygna Castle, he had acquired an exact though unvisualized and unverbalized knowledge of every building and area of the enemy base. And from direct sensation and extrapolation from it, he knew what the base was, and why it was here, and how to enter it, and where to find what he wanted from it.

But it was very hard, after the long intense practice, *not* to use the mind-sense as he approached his enemies: to cut it off, deaden it, using only his eyes and ears and intellect. The incident on the mountainside had warned him that at close range sensitive individuals might become aware of his presence, though in a vague way, as a hunch or premonition. He had drawn the helicopter pilot to the mountain like a fish on a line, though the pilot probably had never understood what had made him fly that way or why he had felt compelled to fire on the men he'd found. Now, entering the huge base alone, Rocannon did not want any attention drawn to himself, none at all, for he came as a thief in the night.

At sunset he had left his windsteed tethered in a hillside clearing, and now after several hours of walking was approaching a group of buildings across a vast, blank plain of cement, the rocket-field. There was only one, and seldom used, now that all men and material were here. War was not waged with lightspeed rockets when the nearest civilized planet was eight lightyears away.

The base was large, terrifyingly large when seen with one's own eyes, but most of the land and buildings went to housing men. The rebels now had almost their whole army here. While the League wasted its time searching and subduing their home planet, they were staking their gamble on the very high probability of their not being found on this one, nameless world among all the worlds of the galaxy. Rocannon knew that some of the giant barracks were empty again; a contingent of soldiers and technicians had been sent out some days ago to take over, as he guessed, a planet they had conquered or had persuaded to join them as allies. Those soldiers would not arrive at that world for almost ten years. The Faradayans were very sure of themselves. They must be doing well in their war. All they had needed to wreck the safety of the League of All Worlds was a well-hidden base, and their six mighty weapons.

He had chosen a night when of all four moons only the little captured asteroid, Heliki, would be in the sky before midnight. It brightened over the hills as he neared a row of hangars, like a black reef on the gray sea of cement, but no one saw him, and he sensed no one near. There were no fences and few guards. Their watch was kept by machines that scanned space for lightyears around the Fomalhaut system. What had they to fear, after all, from the Bronze Age aborigines of the little nameless planet?

Heliki shone at its brightest as Rocannon left the shadow of the row of hangars. It was halfway through its waning cycle when he reached his goal: the six FTL ships. They sat like six immense ebony eggs side by side under a vague, high canopy, a camouflage net. Around the ships, looking like toys, stood a scattering of trees, the edge of Viarn Forest.

Now he had to use his mindhearing, safe or not. In the shadow of a group of trees he stood still and very cautiously, trying to keep his eyes and ears alert at the same time, reached out toward the ovoid ships, into them, around them. In each, he had learned at Breygna, a pilot sat ready day and night to move the ships out—probably to Faraday—in case of emergency.

Emergency, for the six pilots, meant only one thing: that the Control Room, four miles away at the east edge of the base, had been sabotaged or bombed out. In that case each was to move his ship out to safety by using its own controls, for these FTLs had controls like any spaceship, independent of any outside, vulnerable computers and power-sources. But to fly them was to commit suicide; no life survived a faster-than-light "trip." So each pilot was not only a highly trained polynomial mathematician, but a sacrificial fanatic. They were a picked lot. All the same, they got bored sitting and waiting for their unlikely blaze of glory. In one of the ships tonight Rocannan sensed the presence of two men. Both were deeply absorbed. Between them was a plane surface cut in squares. Rocannon had picked up the same impression on many earlier nights, and his rational mind registered *chessboard,* while his mindhearing moved on to the next ship. It was empty.

He went quickly across the dim gray field among scattered trees to the fifth ship in line, climbed its ramp and entered the open port. Inside it had no resemblance to a ship of any kind. It was all rocket-hangars and launching pads, computer banks, reactors, a kind of cramped and deathly labyrinth with corridors wide enough to roll citybuster missiles through. Since it did not proceed through space-time it had no forward or back end, no logic; and he could not read the language of the signs. There was no live mind to reach to as a guide. He spent twenty minutes searching for the control room, methodically, repressing panic, forcing himself not to use the mindhearing lest the absent pilot become uneasy.

Only for a moment, when he had located the control room and found the ansible and sat down before it, did he permit his mind-sense to drift over to the ship that sat east of this one. There he picked up a vivid sensation of a dubious hand hovering over a white Bishop. He withdrew at once. Noting the coordinates at which the ansible sender was set, he changed them to the coordinates of the League HILF Survey Base for Galactic Area 8, at Kerguelen, on the planet New South Georgia—the only coordinates he knew without reference to a handbook. He set the machine to transmit and began to type.

As his fingers (left hand only, awkwardly) struck each key, the letter appeared simultaneously on a small black screen in a room in a city on a planet eight lightyears distant:

> *URGENT· TO LEAGUE PRESIDUIM. The FTL warship base of the Faradayan revolt is on Fomalhaut II, Southwest Continent,* 28°28′ *North by* 121°40′ *West, about* 3 *km. NE of a major river. Base blacked out but should be visible as* 4 *building-squares* 28 *barrack groups and hangar on rocket field running E-W. The* 6 *FTLs are not on the base but in open just SW of rocket field at edge of a forest and are camouflaged with net and light-absorbers. Do not attack indiscriminately as aborigines are not inculpated. This is Gaveral Rocannon of Fomalhaut Ethnographic Survey. I am the only survivor of the expedition. Am*

sending from ansible aboard grounded enemy FTL. About 5 hours till daylight here.

He had intended to add, "Give me a couple of hours to get clear," but did not. If he were caught as he left, the Faradayans would be warned and might move out the FTLs. He switched the transmitter off and reset the coordinates to their previous destination. As he made his way out along the catwalks in the huge corridors he checked the next ship again. The chess-players were up and moving about. He broke into a run, alone in the half-lit, meaningless rooms and corridors. He thought he had taken a wrong turning, but went straight to the port, down the ramp, and off at a dead run past the interminable length of the ship, past the interminable length of the next ship, and into the darkness of the forest.

Once under the trees he could run no more, for his breath burned in his chest, and the black branches let no moonlight through. He went on as fast as he could, working back around the edge of the base to the end of the rocket field and then back the way he had come across country, helped out by Heliki's next cycle of brightness and after another hour by Feni rising. He seemed to make no progress through the dark land, and time was running out. If they bombed the base while he was this close shockwave or firestorm would get him, and he struggled through the darkness with the irrepressible fear of the light that might break behind him and destroy him. But why did they not come, why were they so slow?

It was not yet daybreak when he got to the double-peaked hill where he had left his windsteed. The beast, annoyed at being tied up all night in good hunting country, growled at him. He leaned against its warm shoulder, scratching its ear a little, thinking of Kyo.

When he had got his breath he mounted and urged the steed to walk. For a long time it crouched sphinx-like and would not even rise. At last it got up, protesting in a sing-song snarl, and paced northward with maddening slowness. Hills and fields, abandoned villages and hoary trees were now faint all about them, but not till the white of sunrise spilled over the eastern hills would the windsteed fly. Finally it soared up, found a convenient wind, and floated along through the pale, bright dawn. Now and then Rocannon looked back. Nothing was behind him but the peaceful land, mist lying in the riverbottom westward. He listened with the mind-sense, and felt the thoughts and motions and wakening dreams of his enemies, going on as usual.

He had done what he could do. He had been a fool to think he could do anything. What was one man alone, against a people bent on war? Worn out, chewing wearily on his defeat, he rode on toward Breygna, the only place he had to go. He wondered no longer why the League delayed their attack so long. They were not coming. They had thought his message a trick, a trap. Or, for all he knew, he had misremembered the coordinates: one figure wrong had sent his message out into the void where there was neither time nor space. And for that, Raho had died, Iot had died, Mogien had died: for a message that got nowhere. And he was exiled here for the rest of his life, useless, a stranger on an alien world.

It did not matter, after all. He was only one man. One man's fate is not important.

"If it is not, what is?"

He could not endure those remembered words. He looked back once more, to look away from the memory of Mogien's face—and with a cry threw up his crippled arm to shut out the intolerable light, the tall white tree of fire that sprang up, soundless, on the plains behind him.

In the noise and the blast of wind that followed, the windsteed screamed and bolted, then dropped down to earth in terror. Rocannon got free of the saddle and cowered down on the ground with his head in his arms. But he could not shut it out—not the light but the darkness, the darkness that blinded his mind, the knowledge in his own flesh of the death of a thousand men all in one moment. Death, death, death over and over and yet all at once in one moment in his one body and brain. And after it, silence.

He lifted his head and listened, and heard silence.

EPILOGUE

RIDING DOWN the wind to the court of Breygna at sundown, he dismounted and stood by his windsteed, a tired man, his gray head bowed. They gathered quickly about him, all the bright-haired people of the castle, asking him what the great fire in the south had been, whether runners from the plains telling of the Strangers' destruction were telling the truth. It was strange how they gathered around him, knowing that he knew. He looked for Ganye among them. When he saw her face he found speech, and said haltingly, "The place of the enemy is destroyed. They will not come back here. Your Lord Ganhing has been avenged. And my Lord Mogien. And your brothers, Yahan; and Kyo's people; and my friends. They are all dead."

They made way for him, and he went on into the castle alone.

In the evening of a day some days after that, a clear blue twilight after thundershowers, he walked with Ganye on the rainwet terrace of the tower. She had asked him if he would leave Breygna now. He was a long time answering.

"I don't know. Yahan will go back to the north, to Hallan, I think. There are lads here who would like to make the voyage by sea. And the Lady of Hallan is waiting for news of her son. . . . But Hallan is not my home. I have none here. I am not of your people."

She knew something now of what he was, and asked, "Will your own people not come to seek you?"

He looked out over the lovely country, the river gleaming in the summer dusk far to the south. "They may," he said. "Eight years from now. They can send death at once, but life is slower. . . . Who are my people? I am not what I was. I have changed; I have drunk from the well in the mountains. And I wish never to be again where I might hear the voices of my enemies."

They walked in silence side by side, seven steps to the parapet; then Ganye, looking up toward the blue, dim bulwark of the mountains, said, "Stay with us here."

Rocannon paused a little and then said, "I will. For a while."

But it was for the rest of his life. When ships of the League returned to the planet, and Yahan guided one of the surveys south to Breygna to find him, he was dead. The people of Breygna mourned their Lord, and his widow, tall and fair-haired, wearing a great blue jewel set in gold at her throat, greeted those who came seeking him. So he never knew that the League had given that world his name.